A SET UP FOR REVENGE 2

LILY'S STORY

ASHLEY WILLIAMS

URBAN AINT DEAD

URBAN AINT DEAD
P.O Box 448
Maybrook, NY 12543

Cover Design: Akirecover2cover.com

Edited By: Veronica Miller / Red Diamond Editing by V. Rena, LLC / reddiamondediting5@yahoo.com

Contact Author at FB: Ashley Williams / IG: @authoress_ashley_williams

Contact Publisher at www.urbanaintdead.com

Email: urbanaintdead@gmail.com

Print ISBN: 979-8-9906748-1-3

STAY CONNECTED

To stay up to date on new releases, plus get information on contests, sneak peaks and more,
Click the link below...
https://mailchi.mp/6d21003686d1/subscribe

CONTENTS

SOUNDTRACKS

Scan the QR Code below to listen to the Soundtracks/Singles of some of your favorite U.A.D titles:

Don't have Spotify or Apple Music?
No Sweat!
Visit your choice streaming platform and search URBAN AINT DEAD.

Currently on lock serving a bid?
JPay, iHeartRadio, WHATEVER!
We got you covered.
Simply log into your facility's kiosk or tablet, go to music and
search URBAN AINT DEAD.

SOCIAL MEDIA

Like & Follow us on social media:

FB - URBAN AINT DEAD

IG: @urbanaintdead

Tik Tok - @urbanaintdead

SUBMISSION GUIDELINES

Submit the first three chapters of your completed manuscript to urbanaintdead@gmail.com, subject line: Your book's title. The manuscript must be in a .doc file and sent as an attachment. The document should be in Times New Roman, double-spaced, and in size 12 font. Also, provide your synopsis and full contact information. If sending multiple submissions, they must each be in a separate email. Have a story but no way to submit it electronically? You can still submit to URBAN AINT DEAD. Send in the first three chapters, written or typed, of your completed manuscript to:

URBAN AINT DEAD
P.O Box 448
Maybrook, NY 12543

DO NOT send original manuscript. Must be a duplicate.
Provide your synopsis and a cover letter containing your full contact information.

Thanks for considering URBAN AINT DEAD.

PROLOGUE

I lay on the cold ground struggling to breath. A single tear dropped from my eyes as I stared up into the sky feeling my life slipping away. All I could think about was the life I lived and all the wrong I'd done to so many people. I'd told myself I was going to stay in the house. However, despite what my first mind told me, there I was, allowing someone else to control my actions, and within seconds, my life had been taken from me. As I was crossing over to the other side, I could hear the love of my life calling out to me.

"No… no… why did you do this?"

Lily continued to perform CPR, but I couldn't seem to find my way back to the light, I couldn't wake up. Feeling the warmth of her lips against mine as she blew air into my body, I couldn't retain it. I felt life leaving my body, and there was nothing I could do about it. My hand slipped from inside of hers and I left my woman to grieve.

"Oh my God! Someone please, help me. Call 911. I'm doing

CPR but he's still not waking up." I could hear Lily yelling to anyone around me that would listen.

"Come on, baby, please don't leave me. What the fuck am I supposed to do without you? We got plans, baby, you have to be here for them."

My name was Lillian Haynes, but everyone called me Lily. I grew up in a small town just outside of Mesquite, Texas. I wouldn't say that I came from a broken home because it was only broken because of me. Being a know-it-all teenager, I didn't do well with authority. I wanted to live my own life and figure it out as I went. I came from a two-parent household and was given everything that I wanted. Some would go as far to say that I was born with a silver spoon. I had a wonderful childhood, and if I could rewind time, I would go right back to it.

My mother used to tell me all the time not to rush getting older. But as a hot-headed teenage girl, there was nothing she could tell me that would make me want to stay in a child's place. That was until the day I realized that I would much rather be in my warm bed at home than sleeping out on the streets. However, by that time, I'd wronged my family so badly that they wouldn't even except me back home. That was one of the saddest days of my life, and the day I hit rock bottom. However, I knew I had no one to blame for that but myself.

My parents raised me right. They did as much as they could so that I would grow up to be a wonderful woman. The way I turned out was my own fault. Being on the streets forced me to come up with ways to make my own money. I decided to become a prostitute because I had seen many women make a lot of money from selling their bodies, and money was what I needed. I still got up early in the morning with every intention to do right, but I always found myself going in the wrong direction.

I depended on men, even though I knew better. They saw an opportunity and ran with it, same as anyone else would. When I met my pimp, Jonathan, my life changed, just not for the good. He made me feel love at one point; that was until he started taken from me. What he was doing wasn't right, he wasn't owning up to his part of the deal. It wasn't at all what I signed up for, because he promised to take care good of me. However, I quickly found out that all his promises where lies. He took advantage of me and manipulated me. I put my trust in him and that's all it took for the bullshit to start.

Out of all the females that accompanied Jonathan, I was his favorite one. I ended up letting him get away with too many things, included stealing from me. He owed me, and I was going to get what I was owed.

It took me awhile to find Jonathan and when I did find him, it didn't go as I envisioned it. So much was happening that night that I couldn't get close to him. I saw him sitting out in his car, but before I could approach him, he sped off.

So instead, I sought out revenge on his daughter, Babygirl. Babygirl ended up being just like me in a lot of ways. She just wasn't in the streets the way I was. Babygirl became homeless after being left at a motel to fend for herself by her own father and stepmother. I took that as the opportunity that I'd been waiting for. Babygirl put her trust in me, and I ended up betraying her for my own selfish reasons. I was hurt, so I manipulated Babygirl in the same way her father manipulated me. However, I ended up being caught and ended up with a 10-year sentence.

During my 10-year sentence, I decided to go into the work

release program in an attempt to shorten my sentence. It turned out to be the best decision I'd ever made, because I ended up meeting who I assumed was my better half. Rich was also in the workforce program, but he was on a different level, seeing how he had come from federal prison. His living arrangements were also a lot different than mine. Rich had done a 20-year sentence, but you couldn't tell by the way he carried himself. Rich was in the streets; being a drug dealer was how he ended up behind bars for an extended amount of time.

Rich loved me like no other, he made me feel *special*, it was a feeling that I never felt before. A crazy feeling because sometimes, he made me have weird thoughts. He made my heart ache at times; and sometimes, I didn't know whether it was love or lust. However, what I did know was that I would do anything for my man. Things had started to heat up between Rich and me. We had plans of leaving prison together, going home, and starting a new life. However, this time, I was going to make sure that we did it right. We both decided to move away and leave everything that we ever went through in the past.

I needed Rich, because I had no one else. I had nobody to go home to. Rich talked to a few of his family members, but he didn't have much of his family on his side either. He did, however, have a place to lay his head when he was released, I didn't. The only person in my family that would even take any of my calls was my grandmother. I enjoyed our talks because she always knew how to keep a smile on my face in even my darkest of times. Unfortunately, my grandmother passed away from Covid while I was incarcerated. Covid 19 had taken a lot of my cellmates' families' lives also.

My grandmother was a fighter, she was strong, and I always thought that she would be here forever. I knew that those were only thoughts because we all had to leave here someday. I never got to say goodbye, only over the phone, which wasn't a real goodbye. I only had a few weeks left of my sentence, and I got the news right before I was to be released from prison.

I didn't want to leave prison on the same bullshit and stop the people around me from elevating. By that, I mainly meant Rich. He was my top priority, seeing how he was all I had left. I wanted to make him a better man, but before I could do that, I had to make myself a better woman. Rich, too, was battling with some things and still had some battles to fight. I was going to make sure he didn't do it alone even though he wasn't alone. I wanted to pour into him the same way I felt he poured into me. So, with that being said, any demons Rich was facing, we would be facing together.

Rich had done some unpleasant things that had me doing unpleasant things but together, we made it work. No matter what, I was ridin' out with my man on this mission, no matter how many times he told me *no*. I was in the passenger's seat when my man and I pulled up to the warehouse. When we pulled up to Rich's enemies' location, I immediately felt like Rich had set me up. I quickly found out that the grass was not always greener on the other side. No matter what I changed, I always found myself in one fucked up situation after another.

ONE
BABYGIRL

I sat in the back seat of a police car, heading to a place that I never thought I would be in a million years. I was arrested for murder, but not only murder. I was also arrested for armed robbery. The feeling that was running through me were unbearable. I couldn't believe I was going down for crimes that I did not commit. As I arrived, I looked out of the window, and it wasn't a jail, but it looked like it was a courthouse. After the officers opened the door to let me out, they escorted me up the steps and into the building.

There stood three more officers awaiting my arrival. I was taken into a very small room where one of the officers told me to relax and gave me coffee and donuts.

"Do you need anything?" one of the officers asked.

"No, I don't want to eat nothing, and I don't want to drink anything either," I replied. I was devastated and all I wanted to do was go home.

"Well mam, someone will be with you shortly," the officer informed before walking out of the room.

It wasn't long until two officers dressed in business attire walked into the room, pulled their chairs out, and sat directly in front of me. With their pens and pads in their hands, they placed them both on the table. They both stared at me for about two minutes before opening their mouths to ask me any questions. Saying I was nervous was an understatement. I don't know why I was nervous because I knew I was innocent. Before either one of them could get one word out of their mouths, I spoke first, ending the intense stare off.

"I would like to speak with my attorney first."

"Are you sure you don't want to give us your side? We would love to hear it because right now, all of the evidence points at you," the detective informed, in an effort to get me to speak without my attorney present. They wanted to get as much information as they could so that they could use it against her.

"I'm so sure, I don't want to talk, you can speak with my lawyer."

Those words rolled off my tongue with confidence because I knew I had that recording of Lily confessing to everything; she had set me up and I had all of the evidence. All I needed to do was get it to my attorney and I knew he would chew up all of the charges, I was so sure about that.

"Who's your attorney? We will get him up here," one of the detectives informed me.

"Matt, Matt Sims." I smiled because I had a good ass attorney, and I knew they would know it too.

"Matt Sims?" One of the detectives looked at me with curiosity.

"Yes, Matt Sims," I replied, noticing the way both the detectives looked at each other.

"OK, we will get him on the phone."

My attorney wasted no time coming to my rescue, I could hear him through the door as he walked into the building.

"Where's my client, Cameron Jackson? I need to speak with her."

"Right this way, sir," the female officer escorted him into the small room where I was. My attorney strode in with an all-blue suit, black striped tie, and black Stacy Adams that complimented his suit.

"Cameron," he shook my hand.

"Hello, Mr. Sims," I greeted, wasting no time delivering my lifeline, which was the recording.

"What is this?" he asked in confusion.

"Well, they're accusing me of second-degree murder and armed robbery, but I have Lily, I mean Lillian Haynes, on a recording, confessing to what she did. She was trying to set me up."

"Oh really? Let me just listen to it and we'll get it over to a judge and let him decide, but I'm sure I'll have you up out of here in no time," he winked.

"Thank you, sir," I smiled and felt myself loosening up a little. I knew that my lawyer would do everything to get me out of all charges. Especially now that I had given him the recording I had.

As promised, my lawyer strolled back in about two hours later with the two male officers and told me all my charges had been dropped. They also informed me that they had taken another suspect into custody. As I was walking out of the interrogation room, I saw Lily standing nervously against the wall in handcuffs. I just stared at her, and then she turned around and noticed me.

"What did you do, bitch?" she scoffed.

"I didn't do anything, you did it to yourself. I guess the jokes on you," I replied with a devilish grin. Lily tried to spit on me but missed. I walked out with my lawyer right beside me.

TWO
LILY

"Lilian, you tried it, didn't you? Here we are again, I remember interrogating you a few years ago and you walked away free. Today, you will not be walking away, would you like to give a statement?" the officer spoke.

"Where's Bobby?" I asked.

"You didn't hear? Bobby was arrested for tampering with evidence in the evidence room for one of his hoes to walk scot-free."

"What?" I huffed, not believing what he was telling me.

"Yeah, seems like you aren't the only one he was screwing. Your boy toy will be housed right across the street from you," one of the detective's stated. Causing both to laugh hysterically.

"You want to talk to us or not? We got to get this show on the road," the other detective asked.

"No, I don't," I replied, nonchalantly.

"Okay, suit yourself."

I was taken uptown to the jail where I was booked in for murder and armed robbery.

THREE
BABYGIRL

With Lily behind bars, I felt relieved. Her little plan didn't work, and I would have loved to be a fly on the wall when she found that out. I knew Lily well enough to know that she was on to the next scheme. I was dropped off by my attorney to a nearby hotel. I still didn't know for sure why Christian was arrested, but I could only assume it was due to an old warrant he'd spoken about numerous times. He used to tell me that he was charged with home invasion and aggravated assault awhile back and never went to court for it. *So, maybe that's what it was,* I thought to myself.

I gave him a call to see if he would meet me with some of my belongings. Most of my clothes that were left at his house were brand new with the tags still on them and my shoes were rarely worn. I decided not to take the truck that he gave me, leaving it where it was. In my eyes, the truck was the last thing that tied me to him. Leave it there, and our ties would be cut. I was unsuccessful at reaching him on the phone. My plane was leaving for Atlanta in the morning, so, there was no time to waste. I walked outside of the hotel to flag a taxi, heading to his house, hoping that he would be home.

When I arrived all of his vehicles were there in plain sight. *Hmmmm... I wonder why he didn't answer the phone for me?* I thought to myself. "Please, wait for me?" I asked the taxi driver. He just nodded and continued smoking his cigarette. When I approached the door, it was cracked, and I decided to just walk in. "Christian, are you here?" I yelled throughout the house. I slowly walked through the large home, making my way into the kitchen. I screamed, "What the fuck is this?" Could my life get any worse? I ran out of the house without grabbing anything, jumping in the back seat of the taxi.

"Drive!" I yelled out to the taxi driver.

"Ma'am, what happened? Are you okay?" the driver asked, turning around to look at me. He had his hand on the wheel but had yet to put the car in motion.

"Just drive, sir," I yelled.

I laid my head back on the seat with the vision of Christian's body slumped over his kitchen counter with a bullet in his head. *It's fucked up that someone would do him like that.* I cried to myself as tears rolled down my cheeks. I couldn't believe he was gone. I didn't get to say goodbye, or anything. He was just gone, and I would never be able to speak to him again. That hurt me. Broken up or not, I still cared for him. *I'm leaving Texas for good, and I am not looking back,* I thought.

My cellphone rang, and I looked down to see the word "unknown caller" flashing across my screen.

"Hello?" I answered.

"You have a collect call from ..."

"No, the jokes on you, bitch! Hahahahaha." I heard a voice say in place of her name, and then she hung up.

WTF? Who was that? Lily? I asked myself. I already knew it was her. There was no one else it could be. I couldn't understand why she chose to play childish games, instead of being a woman about her shit.

What has Lily done? I asked myself, wondering why she now thought the joke was on me.

FOUR
LILY

"*Nigga, I will make your life a living hell if you don't give me what's owed to me.*"

"*Bitch, my life is already a living hell, I made you and you're not getting shit!*"

I jumped up out of my sleep with the thought of being choked by the man in my dream. The man that I had been dreaming about for a while now was my old pimp, Jonathan. After being arrested, revenge was all I could constantly think about. Getting Christian knocked off wasn't enough because Babygirl didn't care much about him. Or at least that's what I thought. She had to now it was me that had him killed, especially once I called her after his murder.

I was sentenced to six years hard labor to run consecutive with the four years I had received for the armed robbery charge. Making it a total of ten years, which I did standing on my head. I was also charged with some federal charges, which were dismissed due to lack of evidence. The district attorney's office dropped the second-degree murder charge down to manslaughter because there wasn't any surveillance cameras nor eyewitnesses. With Babygirl refusing to testify against me, manslaughter was the only way they knew I would do time.

The fact that Baby girl didn't even show up to court the day she was supposed to take the stand, showed me a lot about her character. I'd made that woman's life a living hell, and yet and still she spared me. In a way I felt bad for the thing I'd taken Babygirl through. My problem wasn't her, but she'd quickly became collateral damage. She was guilty by association, and I had to get revenge on somebody. So, Babygirl was the next best thing.

I wasn't offered a plea deal for my manslaughter charge, so I knew I would have to take it to trial. I was already seven years into my sentence, and still awaiting trial. With over half of my sentence done I became eligible for the work release program. The program would allow me to work during the day and finish the remainder of my sentence at night. I would need all the money could for when I got out. I had nothing outside these walls for me and would be starting my life all the way over.

I had been seeing a guy named Rich who lived in a halfway house. Seeing how he already had money, he didn't need the work release program. However, one of the rules of the halfway house was that anyone who lived there had to get a job. Job or no job, Rich was a hustler, so he was going to always have money. My new friend was a drug dealer before he got caught up with the feds and charged with drug tracking. So, if need be, he could go right back to what he knew.

He had spent twenty years in the feds and was due to be released in three days, a month before I was to be released. I was sure that I would be moving to Atlanta. Rich was originally from Northeast Louisiana, but he was relocating to Atlanta and had already made plans for me to come live with him.

"Why can't I just let it go? Why am I on this revenge trip still?" I asked myself every day. I want so badly to get Jonathan off my mind, but I just can't let him get away with something like this. I feel played.

After my first attempt to get Jonathan back for what he had done years ago, using his precious daughter Babygirl didn't work. I still had been plotting over the years to make Jonathan pay for what he had done. It might have been minuscule to Jonathan, but it was huge to me. He forced me to have sex with multiple man on for him to take all of my money. I was used to selling myself, but the disrespect was something I could tolerate. He took my money, so for that he had to pay. Jonathan was my pimp and there was an agreement in place. I was supposed to get thirty percent of the trick I had done for Jonathan that night. Needless to say, Jonathan left me with nothing.

I was homeless when I met Jonathan and he had made me many promises and later didn't own up to them. He was all I knew for a long time, and I trusted him and the other ladies that accompanied him too. I was a woman who was all about my cash flow and Jonathan had taken from me and I was still upset about those events that took place many years ago.

I wondered how Babygirl felt when my real age was revealed. I bet she felt stupid and played; at least I hoped. *I hope she felt the same way that I felt and was still feeling,* I thought and smiled to myself.

I'd sent one of my tricks over to Christian's house to take him out. When the job was done, he allowed me and gave me the all clear. Right before hanging up, he let me know that Babygirl had just pulled up to the house. I waited a while and put my burner phone up and used the wall phone. I called to let Babygirl know that the joke was actually on her, and I knew that left her hysterical, and left me feeling like the winner.

I was headed to the shower when I was stopped in my tracks by TT standing by the cell, smiling at me. TT was a stud broad who had long dreads, brown skin, and pretty white teeth. She was everything I loved in a man, only she was a woman. TT had a terrible crush on me since the day I made it to work release. I never gave her a chance because I wasn't really into girls, unless it included getting money. *What the hell? I might as well have the best of both worlds while I'm here,* I thought. I couldn't beat that, but I still played hard to get. She was cute though. I tried to rush past her but was stopped when she grabbed my hand.

"Say ma, I know you see me watching you every time you around, and I know you've been watching me too. Don't act like you're not trying to get with me and explore what I have to offer," TT spoke, while licking her lips.

My panties instantly got wet from what she had told me. I didn't know what to say. I had never been with a girl and didn't know what to do with one. I knew she was experienced and knew what she was doing.

I was open to the idea of been touched by TT, she was a girl, and a girl knew what a girl liked. You would think all of them years out on the streets and working in strip clubs, I would know a thing or two. Nope, I was green when it came to that lifestyle. I wouldn't know what to do, but I blushed.

"Check this out, my love, just take it slow and I won't do anything you're not comfortable with, give me the green light, you tell me when to go," TT said, as she touched me on my nose.

I just stood there, not knowing what to say or do. I didn't know how to tell TT that I wanted her just as bad. TT could tell how badly I wanted her without me having to tell her. My legs trembled. They felt like they were about to give out on me. TT winked at me and started to walk away but looked back at me and saw that I couldn't resist. TT left me leaning up against the wall taking in what she had just said to me. I ran to the shower, not only because I had to go to work, but also because I was feeling juice in my panties.

LILY

I arrived at the casino after being dropped off by the work release van, quickly ditching the other work release girls who also worked with me. I ran to the bathroom to change into something a bit more appealing to the eyes of Rich. Being in prison, I had to still abide by the dress code, but once out of the eyesight of authorities, I was moving like I was free. I put on a pair of black leggings and a cropped hoodie. I graced my feet with a pair of Jordan 97's, applied nothing but eyeliner and mascara to my eyes, and lip gloss to my lips. Before walking out of the bathroom, I quickly wet my hair to bring out my natural curl pattern, before looking in the mirror. "Damn, you look good bitch," I told myself.

"What's up baby? Long weekend, you miss me?" Rich asked as soon as he walked up to me.

"Of course, I've missed you. I can't wait until you get out and the countdown will officially begin for me to be getting out right behind you. Speaking of getting out, you have two more days, baby, and you'll be home sweet home, how does it feel?"

"Man, it's been twenty long years since I had a real taste of freedom and I'm really looking forward to it. Not really looking forward to seeing family because they all fake. But I know my big homies and my oldest son are going to make me feel welcomed once I walk out them gates. Baby, I'm never going back to the streets, I just hope I'm given another chance out there in that world."

Rich didn't speak much about his family; he only spoke about his daughter and two sons. He was really close to his oldest son, but he knew they would all be happy once he was home. On the rare occasion he did speak about his family I could tell he was hiding something from me. Although I wouldn't push him to tell me. I really wanted to know what that something was.

"Awe baby, I wish I could have been able to meet you at the gates with a home cooked meal," I informed him.

"Listen, baby, I just need for you to keep doing what you're doing. I don't need all that extra shit. You loving me is enough."

"You're so sweet. I do love you very much. But what have I been doing that you want me to continue to do?"

"Keeping it real with me and straddling my lap when I want and need it. Matter fact let's go in there and get that poppin' right now," Rich spoke, as we both made our way back to the manager's office.

Rich was just the type of guy that I usually went for in the appearance department. Rich stood around 5'9" in height, with bright skin. I had always had a fetish for thugs with dreads, and Rich embodied that. He was also tall and handsome, and I loved everything about him. He wasn't lacking anywhere and if he was, he sure made-up for it with his nine-inch-thick dick that laid perfectly between his legs. He had juicy lips and a thick tongue that I loved to feel on my kitty. He was also charming and charismatic, but none of that took away from his gangster.

After the quickie that we both had just encountered, Rich grabbed my feet and began to massage them with lotion. Rich knew me very well. So, he knew that after sex I had to have something to eat and a shot of Hennessey. He had already ordered food from his friend who worked at the buffet inside the casino. I loved to eat, but I hated when Rich allowed his friend to come into the manager's office with us. I was already risking my job allowing Rich to be there, so I didn't need any extra bodies.

When Rich's friend knocked on the door, I was startled, so I tried to force Rich to hide under the desk until whoever it was left, but all he did was laugh at me. Quickly letting me know that it was only his friend bringing us the food.

"Thanks bro, thanks for always looking out," I heard Rich telling his friend as he closed the door.

"What are you doing, Rich? We could get caught up like that. We really have to be careful about how we move. You could have easily gone to meet him. Nobody should know we chill in this office. Loose lips sink ships, babe. So, don't bring nobody else back here."

"Chill out, ma, that's just my homie, he'll never rat me out. I'm well respected, believe me when I tell you I got you. You don't have anything to worry about, Queen," Rich assured me.

"I got you a shot of Hen and something to eat, now eat up," Rich continued.

When I opened my to-go plate the smell of seafood instantly filled my nostrils. On my tray were lobster tails, crawfish, crab legs, shrimp, sausage, and two boiled eggs, just how I liked it. I dug in without asking Rich if he wanted any and he just sat there and admired me as I ate my food. I could only imagine the thoughts that took over his mind while he watched me. There was no doubt in my mind that he loved me. The love we shared was untouchable, and nothing or nobody could come between us. Rich was so deep in his thoughts that he didn't realize he had been staring at me for so long, I was starting to think something was wrong with him.

"I'm sorry, baby. I didn't even ask if you wanted any," I spoke, trying to shove shrimp into Rich's mouth.

"Hold on, ma, I'ma gangsta. I don't eat that shit. I eat shit like steak and potatoes. Not no weak ass seafood. I'm from Louisiana true enough, but I don't fuck with it especially since it's not prepared in the boot. We eat that shit on a daily, not for me though, ma."

"You love my seafood eatin' ass, don't yah?" I bragged.

"Hell yeah, I love you and it isn't no denying that."

"Why didn't you get any steak and potatoes? I can't believe you didn't get anything to eat, are you okay, baby?"

"Yeah, I'm good, baby, I wanna see you eat. I'm straight... I survive off making you happy."

"I'ma let you have that corny ass line and keep enjoying my food," I joked.

"Oh, you think what I just said was corny? Damn, that hurt my feelings."

"I was only kidding, baby; I love when you get all sweet on me," I replied, before kissing him passionately.

SIX
LILY

I'd finally made it back to the dorm after a long day's work. Although I hadn't put in much work at my job, I definitely worked overtime, riding Rich like a stallion. I stepped into the hot shower and leaned my head back, allowing the water to run down my neck. I was enjoying my shower when TT stepped in for her shower, startling me.

"Whoa! You scared me, TT."

"What are you scared for? I told you I won't bite you unless you want me to," TT replied, licking her lips. I stepped out the shower and wrapped a towel around my body. I could feel the wetness starting to form between my legs, and I knew what I was about to do.

"Meet me back at my bed when you get out of the shower," I told TT as I placed my hand against her chest.

"Aight, ma."

36

I walked back down to my cell and waited for TT to arrive. I knew she liked me, and I planned to use that to my advantage. I saw the way she looked at me when I touched her. So, I knew I was going to use what I had to get exactly what I wanted. Moments later when TT walked into my cell, I told her to have a seat.

"What do you see in a girl like me?" I wasted no time asking TT.

"So far, I see a beautiful innocent sweet girl. I'm trying to be on your radar more often and get to know the inside of you. I like what I see from the outside, now I'm trying to find out what the inside be like," TT spoke softly.

"How long have you been down?" I asked TT.

"Almost four years. I got about two months left and I'm out this camp. How long do you have left?"

"I got a little under a month left before I go home," I responded.

"What's your plans for when you get out?" TT asked.

"Well, so far, my plans are to move to Atlanta."

"What's in Atlanta?"

"Him," I told her while pointing at Rich's picture.

"His name is Rich, and he gets out in two days. We have so many plans."

"Wait, a nigga in jail?"

"Yeah, what's wrong with that?"

"Niggas in jail only sell dreams. My sister held a nigga down and when he got out he forgot about her and moved on to the next bitch. Then my cousin josed a nigga and the whole time, he was lying about him and his baby mama being together. When he got out of jail, he posted a picture of the both of them together. Come to find out they'd been married the whole time. My other cousin…"

"Wait… stop. I don't want to hear anymore. I don't think Rich would hurt me like that," I spoke, cutting TT of mid-sentence. I knew Rich, and he would never play me the way that TT's cousins had been played.

"Don't listen to me then," TT informed, holding both hands in the air. TT didn't know that I had anger issues, and it was building up, I was about to explode. Just the thought of Rich being with another woman made me want to puke.

"Besides all of that, what do you want from me, TT? You are always so consistent in getting me to talk to you."

"You want my honesty?"

"No, I want you to lie to me, of course I want the truth, TT."

"I want to lick you from head to toe, down to your ankles before inserting my long tongue inside your juice box."

"Damn, is that really what you want to do to me? I've never even been with a female before," I responded.

"You told me that already and I'm not trying to hear that. I want to taste your fine ass and I don't like waiting for what I want. This tongue will change yo life, girl. You better come get you some."

"I have to think about it, TT," I whispered shyly.

"Drop that nigga you are playing with and get with a real one," TT told me, before walking off.

I liked that TT was so persistent. When TT left my bed all I could think about was what she had said about men leaving prison, and the way they treated the women that held them down. I didn't want to believe that Rich would hurt me in any way. I still had to look at the reality of it. Rich had been down for twenty years, and I couldn't truly believe he would come home and be a hundred percent faithful to me. Especially with me still having time left on my sentence. I knew I couldn't force Rich to be who I wanted him to be. All I could do was hope that he wouldn't get out and ruin everything we'd built.

Putting that to the back of my mind and focusing on TT, she had just straight up admitted that she wanted to fuck me, and I liked the energy she'd just brought to me. It wasn't no shame in TT, and I liked that. She knew exactly what she wanted and from the looks of it, she knew *exactly* what to say to get it. I wanted to go jump in the bed with her and let her do her thang and see what she was working with. Instead, I made her wait a little while longer for the kitty.

SEVEN
LILY

Today had been the hardest day at work for me. Rich had gotten out of jail and hadn't called me once. I had been answering every phone call, getting frustrated when it wasn't him calling. I know he hadn't lied to me; Rich didn't seem like that type of guy to lie about something as serious as our relationship. He was a straight up type of man, and I knew that. However, I couldn't get the words TT had spoken out of my head.

"What if it was all a jose to him? What if he was married with a wife waiting for him?" I asked myself over and over.

Just when I was about to call one of Rich's homeboys to see if he was there, I looked over my shoulder and saw Rich walking across the casino floor with a bouquet of flowers, smiling, knowing he was on his way straight to me.

"OMG, baby! I thought you forgot about me… what took you so long to come here? I was waiting for a call or a text from you," I spoke with tears in my eyes.

"Baby, it's only been six hours. I had to go visit some of the few people I fuck with before I fly to Atlanta where my podnuhs are at."

"I know I'm overreacting, I just thought you would forget about me."

"Why would you think that? I told you I'm not like them other niggas you so used to dealing with. We're not the same caliber, so don't compare me, Queen."

"Why can't you just get an apartment out here until I get out? Then we could relocate together when I touchdown. That way you'll be here with me, closer to me."

"You know I have to be back and forth out here anyways to visit my oldest son. That is if he still wants to deal with me. I told you I'm trying to do better for myself this time."

"So, who will you be living with when you land?" I asked, wanting to make sure things were on the up and up.

"Baby, I will be living with my podnuh until you come home. Then we will go find a place together that we both like. I'm not coming back to jail; my old lifestyle is my past now. In order for us to do better we gotta get far away from the streets, and everybody in them. We talked about this already, why are you trying to change the plans now?"

"Baby, you never told me you wanted to stop pushing dope. You know that's what turns me on about you."

"I shouldn't have to tell you that. You should have been able to read between the lines when we talk about our plans every day. I want to do better; I have plenty of money to take care the both of us. I have my welder's license and I'm about to do something with it. I got your back, ma; believe me, I want you *forever*. That's why I bought this ring for you."

"Awe, baby!" I yelled out in surprise, looking at the glistening ring Rich was holding.

"This isn't an engagement ring, just a promise. It's a reminder to let you know that I will always have your back."

"Wow, baby! I wasn't expecting this. I love you so much. You know I got your back in whatever you decide you want to do."

Although I preferred an engagement ring over a promise ring any day, knowing Rich's heart was all mine was good enough for me. I wasn't too thrilled that Rich wanted out of the drug game, but I knew he had plenty of money saved. So, I was with him as long as the money was flowing.

"Now get over here and give your man some love."

I walked over to Rich and kissed him passionately. Still in deep thought about him letting the street life go. I truly loved Rich, however, there was nothing ordinary about our love. I still wanted him in the streets making that fast money. I knew it wasn't right for me to want that from him. However, I was still in survival mode and that's the only way I knew how to live.

I knew it was unfair to Rich, but I didn't know how to let go of my old ways. I was stuck on wanting to pay Jonathan back, and I knew I wouldn't rest until I'd done so. I just didn't want to string Rich along in the game I was playing. I wanted to do the right thing. It was just hard, because my mind was still filled with so much anger, and I wouldn't be okay until it was over and done with.

"Rich, I gotta ask, are you married or got somebody waiting on you to get home? I just feel like you hiding something from me. Like, why are you in such a rush to get back to Atlanta? You got something going on outside of me? I don't even get out for another month. Baby, that's a lot of time to be away from each other. Shit, by the time I get out, you could have started another life with a whole new bitch. I just want to know that truth, because I don't need no surprises when I get home."

"Baby, who have you been talking to? What are you talking

about? We have gone over this multiple times. When will you finally realize I have nobody else and I'm waiting for you? You are all I want and need. What more can I tell you? You have to believe me. When you get out in a month, you will see that I am who I say that I am. I love you."

I smiled because that was exactly what I wanted to hear. I knew that Rich loved me, and he was proving that to me now. However, it was still a bit of doubt in the back of my mind. Although he might not have a wife or girlfriend waiting on him, I was sure that he would dip into some new pussy while I was still locked up. I knew he was a man, and he had needs. So, I wouldn't be too mad if it happened. As long as he wrapped that shit up by the time I got out. I loved Rich too much to just let another woman take him away from me.

EIGHT
LILY

When I made it back to the work release dorm, my housing area was a mess and I immediately walked into the day room and started bucking on everybody.

"Y'all hoes so nasty leaving dirty bowls everywhere, y'all don't like to clean up behind yourselves. Stuff all over the floor and it doesn't make any sense. Half of y'all barely take a bath or brush your teeth. I wonder if y'all man know how trifling you all are living in here but call yourself a bad bitch. Bad bitches clean up and keep themselves up. You hoes not bad, you nasty," I vented, slamming the door behind me.

TT heard the commotion from a deep sleep, she rolled over and saw me rushing back to my area mad as hell. TT got up, went to the bathroom, and brushed her teeth, coming straight to my bedside.

"Yo, what's up with your attitude?" she asked me.

"Nothing. I'm just in a bad mood."

"Just because you're in a bad mood doesn't give you the okay to come in here bringing your bad energy on the rest of us."

"I wasn't talking to you, TT. You don't sleep in my area. Them nasty hoes needed to be set straight. I am so sick of coming in from work to a nasty area. Some of them were off today so there's no reason for their area to be looking torn up and you've been here all day. All my life, I got it out the mud, but I made sure to keep a clean-living area no matter where I would lay my head. And good hygiene. I'm mad and frustrated right now, can we talk later?"

"Naw shawdy, you are comin' up in here throwing temper tantrums and I want to know what's going on with you."

I pulled my hair back into a ponytail and looked at TT.

"I really don't feel like talking about it right now, TT."

"Ok, fine then, don't let that shit keep building up inside of you when you're going through the motions. It's best to get that shit off your chest, ma," TT spoke, before walking away.

I wanted so badly to tell TT about my day. I wanted to tell her about my life and everything I was battling. I felt close to TT. Everything I'd ever told her had stayed between the two of us. I headed for the shower, ready to wash the day off. When I was done, I rubbed lotion all over my body. Then sprayed *A Thousand Wishes* from Bath and Body Works all over my body and went over to TT's bed.

"TT, are you sleep?" I whispered because her bunkies were already asleep, and I didn't want to wake them up.

"No, I'm up, what's up?"

"First, I want to apologize for how I handled you."

"Wait, you didn't handle me so get that shit out of your head," TT Laughed.

"OK well, I apologize for whatever it was, it's just that Rich has my emotions all over the place. One minute, he's in my face claiming that I'm all he wants and giving me a promise ring. Then when I call him, he's not answering any of my calls," I announced as tears flowed freely down my face.

"I know what I said about men who are in jail only be josin' until they get out. I want to apologize for saying that because maybe Rich is just home trying to get his business straight. I never want to come across as trying to bring you down or having you have second thoughts about what you believe in. If you believe in something, you stand on believing in it. That's your man, trust him in the things that he tells you until you have concrete evidence to believe otherwise. I apologize, I should have never got up in your mix the way that I did."

"Yeah, maybe you're right, TT, or maybe you're wrong. As soon as Rich left the casino from being with me all day, I called his phone about 3 hours later because I was concerned about his safety. I called the airport in Atlanta and found out that his plane hadn't landed yet. Then I called back again about an hour ago and was told that his plane landed safely. So, I have been trying to call him repeatedly and I still get nothing. I know he should be settled in by now and even if he wasn't, he should still call to let me know that he is okay. I just don't understand, if he doesn't want me, he should just tell me."

"Just give him some time, he'll come around, if he doesn't come around, you know where to find me," TT joked.

"I hope you are right that he'll come around. Now let's get up and fix us a hookup, I'm starving."

"Me too," TT said. We both got some food items and headed for the microwave.

NINE
LILY

Early Saturday morning I woke up, rolled over, and shut off my alarm clock. I went to the speaker box and told transportation I didn't feel too good today, and I couldn't go to work. I left the speaker box still feeling nauseated. I had been sick for the past three days and my period was late. I decided to stay in while everyone else went to work so I could take a pregnancy test in private. I had snuck off from my job and gotten the test from a corner store just down the street from the casino. I could have gotten in so much trouble for leaving my job, but it was something that I had to get done. The not knowing was eating me up inside, but deep down, I knew the test would come back *positive*. I knew because of the mood swings, going off on my roommates and shit.

I was prepared to stay in from work. So, I snuck my cell phone inside the facility in case Rich called or texted me. As soon as the last crew left for work, I went into the bathroom and took the First Response pregnancy test out of my pocket. Taking a deep breath I sat on the toilet to pee in the small cup. After the process was complete, I sat and waited for the results to appear. After two minutes had passed, I looked at the results and just as I thought, it was positive. However, just to be sure, I waited one extra minute before my final confirmation. Glancing back at the results, they were still the same.

Sitting on the floor against the wall, I didn't know how to feel because I hadn't talk to Rich. *What the fuck have I gotten myself into?* This was supposed to have been a special moment for me. I wasn't feeling it, damn sure not feeling it since I didn't know what's really up with Rich, and being pregnant behind these walls was so uncomfortable, because I knew my man was out there doing me dirty. I had gotten myself into a fucked-up situation that I didn't know how to get out of. Rich hadn't called me or answered any of my calls or texts. I began to worry about what to do and honestly, I didn't know the first thing about being a mother. I paced the bathroom floor for about fifteen minutes straight before going back to my bed.

Picking up my phone and to my surprise, I had thirteen missed calls from Rich and several text messages. I was both excited and mad at the same time. Before I could even call him back, he was calling me again.

"Hello," I answered.

"Baby, I know you mad at me for not calling you but let me explain. Baby, I have missed talking to you. I know you probably think I'm out here on some bull shit but I'm not. Nobody seems to want to hire me because of my background. So, I got back into the game. I've been hustling hard out here getting ready for you to come home to me."

I just held the phone listening to Rich speak his mind. I didn't know rather to curse him out and hang up or give in to him. I definitely gave in, just his voice alone made me melt.

"Rich, I have something I want to tell you."

"Okay baby, let me explain first, it's tough out here. I'm trying to do the right thing, but nobody seems to want to give me another chance to get back on the right path. I know if you were out here with me it would be so much better. I need you out here by my side, you don't have long left."

"I hear you but why you didn't call or text me? You know I would have understood, you know I got your back through anything. You should have told me; you can't keep doing this poppin' in and out of my life. Don't ever do that again because I was so worried about you. I got a few weeks left and then I will be out there with you. You had me in here feeling so alone. I don't know how much more of that I can take. I thought we were better than that."

"Baby, I won't make that mistake again, I know I said it before, I promise I won't. Baby, I have to call you back later tonight after I get this shipment in."

"Be careful out there, baby. I'll be home soon. I love you."

"I love you too."

Rich was up to something; I could feel it and would soon find out what it was. I didn't tell him about my pregnancy yet. He didn't even ask me what I wanted to tell him. I'm glad he didn't bring it back up before he got off the phone, because I realized I really was not ready to tell him. I got out in two weeks, and I wasn't really sure if I was keeping the baby. Covid 19 was getting serious in the world, and Rich also didn't know that my grandmother had passed. She was the one person I knew I had in the world, and now she was gone. Everything was coming down on me at once.

TEN
LILY

Saturdays were always busy for me at the casino, a lot of people came out mainly for the delicious seafood that was sold half off. However, I still managed to text my man every time he texted me. Lately, Rich had been on point with checking in, and I was loving every bit of it. I still couldn't figure out why he would think I would feel some type of way about him being back in the game. Even after I'd told him that's what I wanted him to do.

Something just didn't sit well with me about that. If it was up to me, he wouldn't have even thought of getting out of the game in the first place. I just think he was trying to cover up the real reason he had been missing in action. I stepped outside to catch some fresh air and while doing so, I called Rich to see what he was up to. I felt myself being so clingy and a lot of men liked that from their woman. Not my sneaky ass man though, he rather me not call, and instead, he rather call me.

"Hey, baby! What's good, ma?" he answered on the first ring.

"Oh, nothing, just calling to check up on my man and see how your day was going."

"Shid, I'm having a bad fuckin' day."

"I'm sorry, baby, is there anything I could do to make it better?" I asked, genuinely wanting to know.

"I'm straight, shawdy. Traffic just slow out here that's all. This shit is really pissin' me off because I feel like somebody is steppin' on my toes."

"Slow, you may need to switch lanes, branch out farther, or change the product."

"Naw, shits straight. Niggas so stuck on their suppliers and scared to check this new shit out. I got some fire for they ass. Niggas too scared to fuck with it, but I got a plan though," he informed.

"I just want you to stay safe out there, the streets ain't no joke. I can't wait to be out there with you so I can watch your back."

"That's one of the reasons I fuck with you, shawdy. You keep it solid."

"I will always remain solid as long as you stay true to me, Rich."

"I love you, baby. You think like a nigga, and I sometime have to be careful and remember who I am dealing with. You're not green to this shit by far. My product is good, my supplier always come through and get me straight. Nothing but big shit over here, shawdy, believe that. So far, it's been slow, it will speed up later. It always does," he spoke.

"I'm glad to know that, get that money, baby, but be careful out there. I can't tell you that enough."

"Baby, I'm good. You don't have nothing to worry your pretty little self about."

"I better not," I half joked.

"Baby, could you go ahead and send me the address so I can have that information already put up?" I wanted to know where he was for safety reasons. However, being able to pop up on him and see what was up when I got out would be a plus.

"I will text it to you a day before you get out, ma."

"I really would like to go ahead and get it now because you like to disappear for long periods of time. I have nowhere else to go right now so I'm depending on you, baby," I informed him, laying it on extra thick.

"I'm not going to leave you hanging. I told you that already. I'm not like that, shawdy, I fuck with you tough. Look at your messages I texted you the address, I know you think I have something to hide but I don't. I keep telling you, you are the only one for me."

Looking at my text messages, "Okay, got it," I told him with a smile.

"About yesterday, you said you had something to tell me, what was that all about?" he asked.

"Well, I decided yesterday I would wait to tell you when I got out because you weren't listening."

"I was listening, I listen to everything you say to me. It slipped my mind to ask what it was you had to tell me. My bad, shawdy, I be having a lot of shit on my mind, it slipped, I'm sorry."

"When you are on the phone with me, I should have your full and undivided attention," I stated, seriously.

"You are right, ma, but besides all that, let me know what's up."

"For the past few days, I had been sick, and you know we had been having some pretty passionate sex lately. I was feeling sick the other morning, so I stayed in from work and took a pregnancy test and it came back positive."

"Damn ma. So what you gonna do?"

"Wait, *what*? Aren't you happy?" I asked, confused about his response.

"I'm happy, but we have to get our shit together before bringing another life into this world. Don't you think it's too soon?"

"Fuck no, I don't think it's too soon. We're both getting older, and we are practically in a committed relationship. So, what's the big fuckin' deal?"

"It's not a problem, baby. I apologize I even said that to you."

"No, I'm fuckin' sorry I told you, thinking you would be excited, but boy was I wrong."

"Lily, we're going to make this work. I am happy that we will be having a baby because we both deserve this happiness. This is just the beginning of a brand-new chapter in our life for the both of us. Having a baby wouldn't slow down our progress, I guess."

"Well, you didn't seem too fuckin' happy to me, that surely wasn't the reaction I was expecting. This conversation went beyond how I expected it to go. With that being said I need to get back to work. I will call you later. That's if I haven't scared you with my unexpected news," I doubled back and spoke.

"You know I don't understand you dirty ass men these days. You help make a baby. Y'all love to have unprotected sex knowing that there is a possibility that a baby could be made. When the news is broken to y'all, you act like it was a surprise! Yeah, like I used a turkey baster to trap your ass or something. Everything we did was consensual, and to answer your question about what I'm going to do, I'm keeping my baby, bitch, that's what I'm going to do!" I continued to yell. I was so angry by Rich's response that I didn't know what to do.

"Baby, I'm sorry. That's not what I meant at all. We're both gonna raise this baby together as a family, what you mean?"

I hung up the phone on Rich's trifling ass. Even though I knew Rich didn't mean anything by how he reacted to us having a baby, I still felt some type of way. I was expecting him to be as excited as I was. But whether he wanted to be a part of our child's life or not, I was still going to raise my child and handle my business.

ELEVEN
LILY

It was the day before I was getting out and going home, so I stayed up all night talking to TT on her bunk.

"Aren't you excited I'm about to leave? It's smooth sailing for you, knowing you're leaving after me. I'm just making room for you."

"Yeah, I'm excited that you're leaving but I don't want you to forget about me. I've grown so attached to you. I don't think another woman could ever make me feel the way you have made me feel in this short period of time."

"Don't start talking crazy, I'm not going to forget about you; as a matter of fact, here's my contact info," I offered, reaching into my pocket.

"I wrote it down and had it put up because I knew you were someone I wanted to keep in touch with, use it whenever."

"So, you're really going to Atlanta where dude at?"

"Yes, I have to go where he's at, because I really don't have much of a choice. I don't have any family, TT, and…" I paused.

"And what?"

"It's nothing," I lied.

"Don't start something and not finish telling me what's up."

"TT, sit down, I have something to tell you. It's things you don't know about me and I want to tell you. When I ran away from home, I ended up becoming a prostitute. I got tired of living in a household with so many relatives feeling cramped. I didn't know much about prostitution until I met my pimp, Jonathan. When I tell you that man did me so wrong. He really baited me in by filling my head up with all the lies and had me making so many sudden decisions," I revealed.

"He stole from me, had me doing jobs without paying me. He lied and said he would pay me at the end of the week, and that day never would come. I tried to kill him but the medicine I gave him, didn't do the job. I did some research and found out that the man from off the streets who sold them to me, gave me some sleeping pills that only knocked him out for a few hours. Sadly, he survived the attempt. When he woke up and realized what I had done, he tried to kill me. I woke up the next morning with him gone and all of his belongings. I felt played because his wife Alice was someone I could honestly call a friend at the time. She was one of the ones who understood me, she dipped out on me too. Again, Jonathan stole from me, and I never seen or heard from anyone until a few years later," I continued as I wiped my tears.

"I never could get to him. I lucked up one day and saw him parked at another hotel arguing with Alice. I waited to see what would happen. Surprisingly, what happened next was unbelievable. Alice left the hotel with him and I went to see if anything valuable was left inside that I could get money from. I peeped inside and heard sniffling, and I found out later that he left his daughter at the hotel. Fast forwarding, his daughter Cameron started working at the same hotel I was laying my head at. I approached her, I didn't move too fast because I wanted to make her feel comfortable and more vulnerable to open up to me. I pretended to be a young girl her age who was in the same situation as her. I didn't completely lie because I was really homeless with nowhere to go and no family who cared about me. I only lied about my age. Cameron took me in, gave me a place to stay, and fed me like I was really a runaway teen. My plan worked for a while; I wanted revenge on her father, so I took it out on her instead. That's why I'm here, I was being manipulative, and it backfired on me. Everything that I tried framing her with, I was charged with. I know my reasons for doing what I did wasn't right and I'm trying to do better, but I have no family to go home to. I have to go home to Rich and I'm pregnant, TT."

"Wait, what?"

"Yes, I'm pregnant," I responded with my head down.

"What did Rich say about that?"

"He really didn't give me the response I was looking for. But I know he loves me, and he's going to be a good father."

"Lily, stop making excuses for him, because he doesn't deserve the excuses. He's a grown man. He should have been a man about it."

"Wait, it's really my fault because he was trying to be a man about it. I just wouldn't let him speak after he hurt my feelings, I just hung up on him. I know he didn't mean it."

"I said stop making excuses," TT whispered in my ear, causing wetness to flow between my legs.

"I just want to taste you, girl."

TT planted soft kisses on my neck as she placed her fingers between my legs. She started off with slow circular motions, before catching a rhythm that caused me to moan in pleasure. I grabbed her hand, forcing her fingers deeper inside me, moaning louder.

"You don't need him, Lily," she whispered in my ear.

"Uh TT, why is you fuckin' me like this? This shit is not supposed to feel this good."

I was moaning so loud, I had forgotten where I was. Laying on TT's bunk, not giving a fuck who watched or heard the pleasure I was receiving. I'd never been licked this way before, and I couldn't control the sounds that escaped my lips.

"Ah shit, bitch… you know what you're doing girl, do your thang," I groaned.

TT cupped my size D breast; I moaned lightly while she inserted two fingers back into my wet juice box.

"You so wet, Lily. Squirt for me, baby."

I had never experienced this feeling before. Rich was great in the dick department. However, the way TT was eating my pussy had me second guessing my life choices. When she inserted her fingers inside me while flicking my pearl with her tongue, I lost it. My legs began quivering, sending to have a strong orgasm.

"TT, you made me feel so good," I panted, clearly out of breath.

TT smiled at me with my juices dripping down her lips. That made me smile back because I knew that she had enjoyed this wet, tight, pregnant pussy too.

"You got my number, right?" I asked.

"Yes, I got your number, love bug. And trust me, I will be calling you."

"You better. We will be linking up when you touch down, and round two is on me," I spoke, before licking my lips.

"Ok, bet, may the best man win. Let's see if you are coming how I'm coming. My tongue game official… Rich ain't 'bout shit and I say that with confidence." I just walked away. *Rich's dick game is breathtaking, and TT got that fire head,* I said to myself.

TWELVE
LILY

I woke up in the middle of the night feeling the urge to use the bathroom. Being pregnant had my bladder all messed up. I felt like I had to pee. However, when I sat on the toilet, nothing came out. I quickly became irritated. Leaving the bathroom, I decided to take a detour over to TT's side of the dorm. When I made it over to her bed, I realized she wasn't in it.

Where could she be? It's the middle of the night and she not in her bed? I know she not in the bathroom. It's only one in this dorm, and I was just in it. I thought to myself.

I stood there and thought about it for a second, wondering if TT was in someone else's bed. I didn't want that to be true, but she was a female. A female stud. Studs thought and did things like a real nigga. I got real pissed off inside, thinking that TT was playing me. So, I started going to everyone's bunk. Making the last stop I saw someone with a tent up. The tent was moving a little, so I rushed over to that bed like the mad muthafuka I was. I just knew what I was about to see behind those sheets wasn't going to be eye candy.

When I raised the sheets that was hanging from the bed, there was TT with her face between some girl's legs. I knew for a fact that the bitch was enjoying it. I knew it was good, because I just had it not even three hours ago. When the bitch saw me, you would have thought she saw a damn ghost. TT was still eating the whole plate, not even realizing that I was standing right behind her.

"What the fuck are you doing, TT? Like what's really good? Didn't we just fuck earlier? Now you in someone else's bed. You in here fuckin' her, too? I knew you were a liar; I knew it, there's nothing you can tell me. I don't want to talk to you at all. Don't look so surprised now, you did it. This is hilarious, this is so fuckin' hilarious! You said that I was the only one that you were fuckin' with."

"But Lily…"

"No, don't but Lily me. You're the one that's in the wrong."

"And bitch, what the fuck are you looking at me like that for? You are laying your ass in the bed with my girl, and you still laying there with no fuckin' respect for me or yourself," I continued.

"I'm just sitting here laughing at you because why are you so pressed? That's what's wrong with hoes these days. So quick to check the next bitch. Now, how the fuck was I supposed to know that she was your bitch? She never said anything about her having a bitch, so obviously that didn't matter to her. So, why in the hell would it matter to me? Now get the fuck up out of here before it goes down in this bitch. And another thing, you in here tripping about a whole plastic dick. Yeah, her mouth good and all of that, but you are getting mad over a dick that's not even real. That's lame as fuck," the woman spoke, still laying in her bed.

"You sound really dumb right now, what you mean just a

plastic dick? You loving that plastic dick though. I know you loving it because it's laying right there in between your legs but you talk about me. How in the hell is that lame on my behalf? No, it's lame for you to even let some shit like that come out of your mouth. Now get the fuck up and get the fuck up now," I yelled.

"Listen, Lily, chill out for a minute. I'm the one that's wrong. I fucked up and I need to fix this. So, could you just be quiet for a second and let me just gather my thoughts? It's all my fault. I mislead both of y'all, but Lily, you're not even gay so how can you lock a nigga like me down? You got a *whole man*, and you about to go home in few hours. Why are you coming up in here messing up what I got going on while I'm still here? I thought you understood the assignment. No strings attached and what we had in here is done and over with now. Let's just move on and stick to the plan, what we did was fun, and we will link back up in the free world."

"I understand that TT, it's not even about that. It's the fact that you just got through fuckin' me. Then you in here laid up with the next bitch a few hours later? You couldn't even wait until I leave in a few hours; you could have waited and not did this shit in my face."

"I didn't do the shit in your face, Lily. You put this shit in your own face. Didn't nobody tell you to come walking through here being nosy. You walked up on this shit. You came lookin' for something and you found it. Now, I will hit you up when I touchdown," TT responded.

"Look, I ain't no hater or nothing like that. I'm not feeling this back-and-forth stupid shit. I can't continue to listen to all this between the both of you. I know what I'm dealing with when it comes to you, TT. Lily, you should have known what you were dealing with too, you're not the only bitch she fuckin' with and I'm not either and I'm okay with that. She is hot, look at her. With that being said, I just want to get my head and be out. So, can we just end all this? Lily, could you excuse yourself, please?" the girl spoke, clearly ready to get back to what they were doing.

"Oh, I'm going to excuse myself alright, you disrespectful lookin' troll."

Before I knew it, I was all over that bitch. She got up and I was knocking her ass right back down. I'm not sure why I was so angry. I knew TT wasn't my girl. Hell, I wasn't even gay. On top of that, I had a whole nigga waiting on me at home. But that head had me gone, so fuck that bitch.

"Get the fuck off me, stupid bitch! Somebody press the fuckin' button," the girl yelled out.

The lights came on and everybody stood around watching me drag that bitch through the dorm. Nobody pressed the button for the C.O. to come and save her little bitch ass. I heard a bitch yell, 'Beat her ass Lily, that hoe deserve it.'"

Somebody else shouted, "You doing what I always wanted to do when I caught her fuckin' my bitch."

Another person hollered, "That slut had it coming."

I beat the bitch's ass so bad, and all TT did was stand there and watch. I knew she didn't give a damn about that bitch because she stood there laughing. I stopped beating that hoe, feeling sorry for the way I'd just slaughtered her. The bitch wasn't even fighting back. When I let her go, I began feeling lightheaded and the next thing I knew I was hitting the floor.

THIRTEEN
LILY

"Lily, wake up, are you okay?" I heard someone ask.

"I'm okay, what happened?"

"Baby, you were in a fight because you caught a bitch in my bed and spazzed out. This shit is all my fault. Please tell me you're okay," TT spoke, standing over me.

"I got into a fight because of you? Damn, that shit must was really serious to get me out of my character."

"You don't remember shit?"

"Hell yea, I remember whoopin' that bitch ass for disrespecting me. Not because she was playing around in bed with you. Respect is not to be disrespected and that's one of the mottos I will always stand on."

"You out here wildin', that shit not good. And you about to leave me behind. There you go being selfish, and I told you about that shit."

"How is that being selfish? I'm not even gone yet; I was claiming what I thought was all mine for the time being. I guess I was wrong though."

"I apologize for waking everyone up, y'all can move around now, I got it from here," TT spoke, before watching everyone in the dorm scatter.

"My bad TT, I flashed out and I shouldn't have done that. That shit makes me look like a damn fool and I feel bad about it. That head shouldn't be so damn good. Make a bitch act up behind it. I ain't gone stunt, I spazzed behind that plastic dick and irresistible hard tongue. That shit had a bitch fucked up in the head for a minute. But I'm good now. Can you help me up though? I think I did too much, I'm cramping," I continued.

"Lily, you're bleeding," TT pointed out as she helped me to my feet.

"Bleeding? Nah, it ain't no blood, I'm just cramping," I replied.

"There's a big blood spot on the back of your pants. Lily, go to the bathroom and check yourself out."

I made it to the bathroom and before I pulled down my pants, I felt a gush of wetness squirt from between my legs. Pulling my pants all the way down, the blood was flowing out of me like water. So, I knew whatever was going on was much more serious than just a few cramps. Sitting down on the toilet, it instantly filled with blood within seconds. I was losing a lot of blood, which probably explained why I fainted. I held tissue between my legs while I walked to the sink. Not knowing what to do, I tried drinking as much water as I could, in an effort to keep myself hydrated.

I began feeling too weak to stand, so I sat back down on the toilet. I pressed my stomach and could hear blood clots drop into the toilet. I was devastated knowing I was losing or about to lose my baby. My karma was coming down on me hard. All I could think about was what I was going to say to Rich. How could I tell him that I lost our baby fighting over a bitch I wasn't supposed to be fucking in the first place? This shit was all my fault, and it was fucked up. In that moment I had forgotten that I was pregnant and put my baby's life at risk. I sat on the toilet crying, wishing this night had never happened.

"Fuck TT, you scared me!" I yelled out. Looking up to see TT right in front of me.

"You straight?" she asked with concern in her voice.

"I'm not straight, I believe I lost my child and it's all my fault."

"Why do you think you lost the baby? Is it because of the blood?"

"It's not just a little bit of blood, it's a lot. And I'm clotting. My luck isn't so good right now; karma is haunting me."

"It will all play out for your good. I'm sorry for what happened. Be careful out there and know that I got love for you."

"I got love for you also, that's a part of the reason I acted out like that." TT didn't say another word as she walked out the bathroom.

I knew I had miscarried my child when the biggest blood clot that I had ever seen dropped into the toilet. Stuffing toilet paper into my panties I pulled up my pants, knowing the tissue would have to due until I was able to get a pad. I walked out of the bathroom with sadness in my heart. I staggered back to my side of the dorm, beating myself up at how stupid I'd been. Because of me, my baby wouldn't even get a chance at life. All I wanted to do was lay down and cry. However, when I got back to my dorm, a girl confronted me I had only seen around a few times.

"Bitch, I don't condone that silly shit you did to that girl. She was just doing what all these other hoes do. You should have been mad at the one person who didn't keep it real. First, you set an innocent girl up for your own pleasure and it backfired, landing you in here. Now you are bullying another innocent situation. Just because things don't go your way doesn't mean you have to always take action. That girl is badly hurt and you walking around with no care in the world," the girl spoke firmly.

"Ma'am, mind your business," I replied, before walking to my bed.

FOURTEEN
LILY

After everything that happened earlier that morning, I was so happy that it was all over. I was finally about to be a free woman. Although I was still sad about losing my child, I was happy that my days behind the wall were behind me. I didn't fall back asleep; I was too anxious. I heard my name being called to be released. Everyone spoke their goodbyes, letting me know how much they would miss me. While others told me to make sure I never had to come back.

"Y'all better not be sayin' my name around this muthafucka. I'm superstitious about that shit. Say a muthafucka's name around here and they ass will be right back," I informed them, causing them all to burst out into laughter.

"TT, you better call me. Don't leave me hangin' just cause I'm outside."

"I got you. I damn sure ain't gon' forget about you," she replied.

"Goodbye, y'all," I called out to them as I walked to the door.

Once I made it out the gates, I took out my phone to check the time, it was almost nine in the morning and my plane left for Atlanta at ten. I called for someone to come pick me up from the gates. I was feeling sad because I wanted Rich to pick me up, but he was so far away. I wanted so badly to have a family waiting for me like the rest of the girls did.

"Hello," the lady answered.

"I'm located at the Dallas Transitional Program for Women, and I need a cab to take me to the airport by 10AM."

"Okay, yes ma'am, your driver will arrive in fifteen minutes. That'll be plenty of time to get you safely to your destination."

"Thank you, ma'am."

The driver wasn't playing any games, he got me to the airport fast. I didn't even have time to rest my eyes like I'd planned to do. Arriving at the airport, I slid my credit card in the machine to pay before getting out of the car. I walked into the airport since I had already paid for my ticket online. After checking in and securing my flight, I sat down, reading a magazine until my flight was announced. Feeling a tap on my shoulder, I turned around and couldn't believe who I was seeing.

"Jonathan?"

"Yes, it's me." He smiled sinisterly.

"Wait, how did you even find me?" I asked in confusion.

"Just like you, I can and will *always* find you. I called the D.O.C. hotline awhile back and got your release date. I waited outside this morning for you to come out and leave and followed you here."

I was in shock. I couldn't believe Jonathan was standing right in front of me. All this time I'd been looking for him, and here he was in the flesh. I had to admit, I was a bit nervous because I knew exactly what he was capable of. He took a seat beside me before he continued to speak.

"I just want to squash all of this now that you're out of jail. I want everything to continue going smoothly. I want you to leave my daughter alone, she didn't deserve any of this. I'm the only one you should be mad with."

"Jonathan, I don't know what you're talking about, I'm not going to mess with your family. I can care less about that. Besides, you weren't thinking about your family when you took from me. You left me with nothing. That's why the pain is personal."

"I want you to take this," he replied, throwing a wad of cash into my lap.

"There's your money. That's all I owe. Take it and please leave my daughter alone."

"Oh, I'll take the cash, but leaving your precious daughter alone will not be happening."

I walked away from Jonathan, leaving him sitting there. I knew him well enough to know that walking away and being silent were his pet peeves. I knew it bruised his ego not knowing what my next move was going to be.

I was ready to board the plane. I had been ignoring Rich's calls and texts because I didn't want him to know I was on my way. I had told Rich that my flight was leaving the next morning, so I planned to call him once my flight landed. I just had to make a stop first. Although I had been in prison for the past five years, I still had an addiction problem that I was still battling with. The time I spent in work release made it easy for me to get high during incarceration.

Since I wasn't pregnant anymore, I was ready to get high. I had already spoken with my friend about coping some coke when I landed. So, it was all set up. I felt so bad because I used to give advice about doing drugs to the women in jail. They would even do drugs while pregnant. They would come to jail pregnant and end up giving their child up to a stranger because they had no other family to contact. Now I was doing what I preached about.

I couldn't help the urge that I had for coke, I wanted to beat that addiction. When my plane landed in Atlanta I immediately contacted my old friend and met him at a coffee shop that was right across the street. I spotted him standing outside of the shop, and he gave me the two-finger signal. *Home sweet home,* I thought to myself, referring to the coke. Rich thought I was new to Atlanta; I wasn't new at all. I just made Rich think that because he didn't need to know everything. I knew everything about Atlanta, I was very familiar with a lot of places due to my past life.

Jogging across the street, I grabbed the plastic bag from the newspaper machine. My friend had set it there before walking away, making the transaction go smoothly. I walked into the coffee shop and headed straight to the restroom. Venturing inside one of the stalls, I took out a long line of coke and snorted it quickly. I was at a high that I hadn't felt in a long time. *After all the time I spent in jail, I still hadn't changed and that's a shame,* I said to myself. I didn't get out and do right like I was supposed to.

FIFTEEN
LILY

I arrived at the address that Rich had given to me high as hell. I stood there, knocking at the side door just to get no answer. Me being me, I twisted the knob and the door opened. I was now standing in the living room of Rich's homeboy's townhouse. Something wasn't right, I could feel it. I knew Rich was in that house doing something and I was about to find out what it was.

I crept up the stairs and I heard loud, passionate moaning coming from a man and a woman. The familiar voice coming from the man's groans sounded like Rich and I lost all understanding. When I opened the door, my high faded after I saw the girl, correction - two girls. My man was laying in the bed with not only one bitch, but two bitches. I didn't know what to do as I stood there speechless.

I never thought in a million years that I would be witnessing my man getting pleasured by two bitches. One bitch was ridin' that nigga's face like there was no tomorrow. While the other bitch rode his dick like she had a point to prove. They were so into it, they didn't even see me standing in the room with them. They were getting ready to switch positions when the little freak hoes finally turned and noticed me before Rich did.

"Oh, hi, you came to join us?" one of the hoes asked while kissing the other bitch in the mouth. Rich turned and looked to see who she was talking to and hopped up like he wasn't already caught.

"Na, gone finish. Don't stop now, I'm not here to spoil your moment. I came to surprise you and looks like I'm the one that got the surprise."

I stared at the two pretty bitches that were on the bed. Not saying that they looked better than me, but they were cute, and I gave credit where credit was due. I just couldn't believe that my man was in here fuckin' two bitches. So, I circled the bed, looked around a little bit, and did the unthinkable.

"This what you want, huh? This what you in here doing?"

They all just looked at me, not knowing what to do or think. "Don't stop now that I'm here. Y'all wasn't thinking about me before. So don't think about me now. You wanna suck his dick, bitch?" I asked, looking over at one of the girls. When she didn't speak I walked over to the bed.

"You was just fuckin' my man like he was yours. Now you scared to put his dick in yo mouth. Stop playin' and suck his dick."

"Lily, what are you doing?" Rich asked in confusion.

"I'm just giving you what you want. You wanted to fuck these two bitches right? Well, I wanna watch. Now like I said, suck his dick," I ordered. Turning my attention back to the girl.

Doing as she was told, she slid Rich's dick back into her mouth. I could hear her slurping noises as Rich starred into my eyes. He grabbed the back of her head, licking his lips while never breaking eye contact with me. When I told the other bitch to sit on Rich's face, she did so without any hesitation. If I didn't just suffered a miscarriage, I would have beaten the shit out of all three of them for playing with me.

However, I felt bad that I'd just sacrificed our child to fight for another woman. I was doing the same thing that Rich was doing only mine came with much bigger consequences. So, this time and this time only, I would let him have this. I sat in the chair across from the bed and watched the show they were putting on. I gave the ordered while they did the fucking, and I could tell my man loved it. I told Rich that I wanted to watch him fuck them both, he quickly got up.

Pulling the girl who was just sitting on his face to the edge of the bed, he opened her legs wide before he entered her, and the moan he let out caused my nipples to harden. As much as I wanted to get down with the action, I knew I couldn't. I was still sore and bleeding, so all I could do was watch. When it was over I looked Rich in the eyes before asking him if he'd gotten what he wanted. He immediately told the girls to leave and waited for them to walk out before speaking again.

"I'm sorry, baby. I ain't mean for you to walk in on that. I thought you would call me when you landed."

"So, because I ain't call you that mean go find two new bitches to fuck?"

"No baby, that's not what I was saying."

"Why Rich? Why did you cheat on me?" I asked.

"Look Lily, I'm sorry, baby. I really was just keeping them around because I was lonely. I don't want nobody else but you, baby, please forgive me," Rich pleaded, looking me in the eyes.

"This was your distraction? Are they the reason wouldn't answer my calls or texts? You know how hurt I am, why men do this shit? It's hard enough already for me to trust and do right. You out here doing me like this? I'm so sick of cheating men… I don't deserve this shit! Rich, I had your back when nobody else did, I was your backbone. So, I thought after all that we been through, we had a serious bond. I only wanted to be released to a good man waiting for me."

"I am a good man, Lily. I messed up thinking with my dick, that's all. That don't make me a bad guy. That just means I'm human and made a mistake."

"That don't make you a good man, you would have kept it inside your pants." I pointed to his dick. "I can't believe you did this to me!"

I was yelling at the top of my lungs. Due to my past, I was still dealing with some demons and Rich didn't make it any better. I wanted him to be my happy ever after along with the baby that I had lost.

"Calm down, Lily, you're carrying my seed."

"Oh, now you worried about your baby? But you weren't too thrilled when I told you I was pregnant, why are you so concerned now?" My face was soaked with flowing tears, my makeup was running, and I was looking a mess.

"Baby, don't leave me; I need you here with me," he pleaded.

"Leave you how? I don't have any family and you know that. I came out here for you. For us and our family that we are building. You laid up in here with bitches wasn't worth it, was it? Take your ring back," I pulled off the ring and threw it at him. I wanted to hit him in the face, but I decided against it.

"I'm not into dreams, you can't sell me dreams, Rich. I'm not buying them. I'm hurt, but I have no choice but to stay right here with you. I have to stay with you, you're the only man who has understood me. I have to be with you, I feel like you complete me."

"I need you as much as you need me, Lily. I don't want the ring back. I'm addicted to you."

Falling into Rich's opened arms I whispered, "I love you." From there, nothing else mattered but us. Now all I had to do was tell him that I'd lost our baby.

SIXTEEN
LILY

The next morning Rich walked into the bedroom where I was sleeping and in my sleep I heard him telling me how sorry he was for breaking my heart. When he sat down beside me, my eyes immediately opened. Feeling the tightness in my eyes, I knew they were still red and swollen from crying all night.

"I didn't mean to hurt you, Lily. Please believe me when I tell you I only want to be with you. Those other hoes don't mean shit to me. We are too deep to be mad at each other." Rich thought he was making the situation better, instead he was only making it worse.

"You don't love me like I thought you loved me, Rich, just please leave me alone for a while. I need some time to think."

Rich got up and headed for the door while I stayed in bed. I stared at the ceiling, thinking how things could get any worse for me. Within minutes, I saw just how bad things could get. I constantly felt wetness between my legs, and I had been cramping on and off all day. I had never been pregnant before, so I didn't know what was normal or abnormal. I called out to Rich a few times, but he didn't answer me. I walked to the bathroom, barely moving.

I made it to the toilet, pulled my pants down, and saw so much blood that my head started to spin. It felt like I was living the nightmare again from going through the same process that I just went through a couple nights before. I felt like I had to pee, but it was not my bladder. I cried more and more; the pain was unbearable. I knew I should have gone to the hospital, but I thought about the coke that was in my system and decided against it. At that moment I knew I had to tell Rich that I had lost our baby after finally hearing him walking past the bathroom door.

"Are you okay? Why are you still crying? I'm not going to cheat on you anymore, baby, I promise."

"Rich, I'm not crying about that weak ass shit you pulled yesterday. I just lost our baby."

"Oh my God, Lily. Shit! What happened?"

"What you mean, what happened? You were caught laid up with two bitches is what happened, and you know that shit, don't act dumb."

I knew when I told that lie, I was wrong for blaming him, knowing that he wasn't the cause of my miscarriage. I just didn't have it in me to tell him that I had been cheating, too. And as a result I had lost our baby. I know it was selfish, but I just could tell him the truth.

"What they got to do with anything?" Rich asked, dumbfounded.

"I was stressed out behind what I thought was love, but instead, you cheated on me. I walked into your space trying to surprise you and you was in here fuckin' two bitches. I get pissed off thinking about this shit. I knew it was in you, I just didn't want to believe it. I wanted it to be only my imagination. Dammit Rich, that was my first baby! You know how long I've waited to have a child? I'm not young."

"I feel bad, Lily, but you can't blame it all on me because you know you still be doing coke."

"What did you say to me?" I asked, shocked.

"Yeah, you must didn't know I knew my podnuh was bringing you that shit. I still accepted you, flaws and all. He would always tell me he was coming up short when he sold it to you. Finally, one day, I caught you myself. I caught you in the back at the casino where my podnuh kept his shit at. You opened that locker and took some of his stash. You were so fast and smooth with it, I knew from that day forward to watch you. I always knew I had a beast ridin' with me. I just never judged you and knew things would get better. I knew that it would, at least that's what I told myself. I knew you were still doing it when I left. I'm trying to get you to see that I'm not perfect and you're not perfect either. Not saying what I did was right because it wasn't right at all. Just please forgive me, Lily, we must help one another cope with losing our child."

"I know to forgive you is to forget but I don't think I'm ready to forget what you promised to never do to me."

"But will you stay here with me so we can at least work it out?" Rich asked.

"I told you I don't have any family; I don't have a choice."

"I don't want you to leave when you do have a choice though, Lily."

"We will discuss that when that time comes, one step at a time," I revealed. Honestly, I didn't know what I was going to do. I loved Rich and I knew he loved me. However, I couldn't help but take the loss of our child as a sign from God.

SEVENTEEN
LILY

It took me two months to forgive Rich for cheating on me, but I had done so. We were now in a much better space in our relationship, and I couldn't be happier about it. We were both now living together in our own place. Making our relationship work the way we'd planned. For the first time in a long time, I could honestly say I was happy. I walked downstairs one afternoon to find Rich sitting in the living room on the sectional. At first glance, I thought he was sleeping, until I got closer.

"What's wrong, baby?" I asked.

"I'm just thinking, that's all."

"Thinking about what? Are you up to talking about it?"

"It's my cousin, Lily. You know I never really explained the details to why I was in prison for years. Yes, I was in there for some drug charges from Louisiana. But that only came up when they came to my house to arrest me for a murder case in Texas."

"Let's talk about it, baby, get it off your chest," I spoke, attempting to comfort my man.

"Well, my oldest brothers, P Dub and Big L, introduced me into the drug game at a young age. We had an organization called "Money Lovers Incorporation," which was only ran by my cousin KH. Shid, KH had shit on lock throughout the whole state of Texas. I was still young and learning, so my big brothers taught me the game which was taught to them by KH. Me and KH were both hanging outside one of our trap houses one day when an all-black on black Altima pulled up. Them muthafuckas started blasting on us and KH was hit in the process. Everybody came out of the house and started blasting but it was too late. The Altima had gotten away. I was hurt to see my cousin laying out, not moving or breathing. Ever since that day, Lily, I felt like it was all my fault."

"How was it your fault, Rich? I don't understand, you both were just hanging outside… neither of you were expecting those killers to do a drive-by."

"Yeah, but Lily, I was right there beside him. They caught me slipping without my piece and I should have had it on me. Even if he couldn't get to his piece in time, I should've been able to get to mine. That's how the game was supposed to go, but I didn't have it on me. Why didn't I have it on me? I still don't know and that's why I feel bad about the situation, it's fucked up."

"I understand your pain, baby, trust me, I understand. So, what do you want to do about it?"

"You see why I love you so much and don't ever want to lose you, baby? Because you are a rider for your man. Look at you already ready to jump into action. But this one is not your fight, ma, let me take care of this one."

"I know but let me have your back on this… I know how to move too, Rich."

"I'm very aware of what you are capable of, but no, Lily. I'm not about to put you in harm's way or any situation to have you put back into jail."

Man, isn't he a different breed? Any other nigga would have let me go with him with no questions asked. Probably would have even blamed it all on me when shit hits the fan. I thought to myself as I smiled at him.

"So, what's your plan?" I asked.

"Shid, I popped one nigga the same night after the shit happened. I slipped up and didn't make sure the nigga was dead right then. Nigga ended up telling the police it was me at the hospital right before he died. There's two more to go, and I've been watching their every move. They're pretty smart when they move, they must be big timers now. The drug game must have treated them well because their whip game sick. They always got security around them, too. But either way, I'ma get them niggas."

"If they have security following them, how do you plan to get around the security?"

"During the day they only have one big nigga following them. I'm just going to lay his big ass down first."

"During the day?" I asked, confused.

"Yeah, I got it covered, they meet at an abandoned building, which is the perfect spot to go with my move."

"Sounds like a plan to me, you know I got your back no matter what."

"I know but stay out of this one, this could get too dangerous."

I was hearing Rich but wasn't listening to him at all. I had and always would have Rich's back no matter what he said. So, if he was riding out, so was I.

"So Rich, baby, you never mentioned where your brothers were at now."

"Shid, they around. I haven't talked to them in years though," he said sadly.

"That explains why you never really talked about your siblings; it was always your homeboys being discussed."

"Yeah, my podnuhs the only ones that kept it G with a nigga throughout my jose. Even though I don't fuck with my brothers and may never talk to them again, I still feel like I owe them my street loyalty. And after this shit I pull off, I know the streets gone talk and my bros gone know I was responsible for the action."

EIGHTEEN
LILY

I stood in the kitchen cooking dinner when Rich walked inside. I was glad to see him because I felt we needed to have a conversation. I'd been thinking a lot about what Rich told me about the murder of his cousin. I knew he wanted to get at the niggas that killed his cousin, and as his woman, I wanted to help him. Revenge was my lane, and no matter how many times he said he didn't need my help, I knew he did.

"Damn baby, you got it smelling good as hell in here," Rich complimented.

"I'm just in here trying to hook something up for us real quick. I wanna talk to you about something, baby."

"What's on your mind?"

"I need to help you get them niggas. I been in the streets for a long-time, baby, and I know what I'm doing. Trust me, two heads are always better than one."

"I already told you that I don't want you getting in no trouble. Besides, what I look like takin' my woman out on a mission?" Rich responded.

"You not takin' me nowhere, I'm riding with you. We on our Bonnie and Clyde shit. Let's show these niggas what's up."

The way Rich smiled at me let me know he was gonna let me come with him. So, over dinner, we talked about the many different ways we could make it happen.

The next day I watched Rich as his icy white BMW came to a slow creep right outside a gated community. He parked on the corner so that his targets wouldn't see him. We had followed them until they led us back to their homes. Tiger and Jon-Jon were the last two of Rich's cousin's killers and neither one of them knew that their days were numbered.

I was parked behind Rich in a black SUV, watching his targets just as hard as he was. I was ready to go to war for my man, and I was going to have his back by any means. I picked up my phone and called him.

"Yo," he answered.

"I love you, baby. We bout to get these muthafuckas together," I spoke proudly.

"I love you too, baby. These niggas ain't even gon' see it comin'."

"I can't believe yo down ass came with me. This the realest shit ever to a nigga like me," he continued.

"You the realest nigga ever to a bitch like me. I'ma always ride out with you," I replied.

"And I'ma always ride out for you too, Lily."

"What's next?" I asked.

"We going back to the house."

"The house? Why?" I asked, confused.

"Now that we know where these niggas live, it's time for us to plan our next step."

"When we going back to get them niggas?" I asked as soon as we walked into our front door.

"Look at you, willing and ready. We're still peepin' shit out right now. We gotta go back to that spot again tomorrow night, I just found out that's Tiger's spot. But that nigga Jon-Jon was over there too. Something is up with them fuck niggas and we gonna find out. Them niggas movin' some major shit, I can feel it."

"Why we gotta peep the shit out? Let's just walk up in that bitch like we Bonnie and Clyde and handle that shit on site."

"Naw baby, this gotta be calculated and done the right way, we cannot fuck this up. When you are doing dirt, you can't go blind. I had to learn the hard way, and I'm sure you have had a lesson or two. I have to do it this way because once I take them fools out, I'm gonna take all their drugs and money. I want the whole stash. No mistakes is the key factor, Lily, so let's move slow. I want the spot where the most drugs and money is being stashed, we gotta do the this shit the right way. We gonna get revenge and come up off a big lick. They already fucked up when they let me follow them to their spot. I wonder who this nigga is that's on payroll for them because that nigga trash. He let me follow them all the way across town… at first, I thought it was a trap until they pulled into the neighborhood. So, let's just follow them a few more days just to make sure we haven't missed anything. Tomorrow we'll take the Jag, and we will keep switching whips and jumpin' in rentals until we get their every move down pack and cover any loose ends. No mistakes, that's all you have to remember, you got me?"

"I got you, baby. I got this under control," I said, smiling.

"Now come over here and give me some love," Rich requested.

When we embraced each other one thing led to another. Making our way to the bedroom. It had been a while since we'd made love, and my body needed it. Rich kissed me down my neck until he got to my breasts. He began sucking on my nipples softly, causing me to moan. I laid on the bed, opening my legs so he could taste me. I moaned as soon as his wet tongue breezed across my pearl. We made love for the rest of the night, falling asleep in each other's arms afterward.

NINETEEN
LILY

Rich and I both had to go and see our parole officers the next morning, just to check in. We chilled for the rest of the day. Later that night we went looking for the opps. Rich and I had been riding around to all of the spots he knew Jon-Jon and Tiger frequented. However, we came up empty handed.

"So, what do we do now?" I asked Rich.

"We wait," Rich responded. "We wait until I get the call back from my podnuhs who also got eyes on them." As soon as the call came through Rich didn't hesitate to answer.

"Yo, what's the word?" Rich spoke, putting the phone on speaker.

"Come to Bankhead at the little spot we normally meet at." He told Rich.

"Bankhead?"

"Yeah nigga, I will explain the shit to you when you get here."

Rich ended the call and looked over at me.

"We are about to go to Bankhead, something is up. That was my lil' podnuh, he said he would explain everything to me once we got there."

"What's up, boy?" Terrance and Mario dapped Rich up as soon as we exited the car.

"What the deal is? I'm anxious to know wassup."

"We found out them niggas got a bigger stash spot than the one they had before. That shit right around the corner, " Mario pointed.

"Real talk? Them niggas must be doing good as hell. I know which building you're talking about and it's big as hell. They must have so much supply that it wouldn't fit in that small spot they had before. Them niggas better play it safe and eat good because soon it will be lights out for both of them," Rich spoke.

"Yo, what's up with your girl ridin' around with you?" Mario asked Rich.

"You know how trill she is, I told you about her. She wanted to ride with me on this shit; I told her what I had done to get them twenty years. She for sure wanted to show some love on this project, she been locked up for some shit too. I explained to her the seriousness and the consequences of the whole thing, and she wouldn't take no for an answer. So, here we both are out looking to seek revenge on these clowns. Lily hasn't left my side even though I really wish she would."

"Damn that's deep. Ol' girl got your back, but we do, too. You know whether you do this shit with or without us, we are coming through smashing shit on sight," Terrance assured.

"I know, son. Man, this is the moment I been thinking about the whole time I was behind them walls. Knowing them niggas were still out here breathing made me sick to my stomach every day."

"Shid, them niggas were out here breathing because you chose for them to breathe. You know we would have taken the both of them out on command," Terrance said.

"I know how loyal the both of you are and without hesitation, I know y'all would have stretched them on sight. But I wanted to be the one to see them take their last breaths just like I had to see my cousin take his last breath. I want their deaths to be torture and I want to be the one to do it."

"Say less, that's understandable and that is why we are staying out of the way unless you need us to handle something," Mario informed.

"Alright, let's get going, I got some stuff to go take care of."

"Aight, bruh bruh, we will get up with you later. Be safe out here in these streets and keep us updated on your moves," Mario said his goodbye.

They both dapped Rich up, and he got back into the whip where I was waiting.

"Is everything okay, baby?" I asked with my Glock sitting on my lap.

Rich laughed and replied, "Everything is everything. I'll explain to you when we get home."

TWENTY
LILY

Soon as we arrived home, I wasted no time in asking Rich what was going on. I'd heard him and his boys talking but couldn't make out everything. I knew whatever it was, it was serious. So, I needed to know firsthand.

"Baby, what's up with the move?" I asked.

"Shid, them niggas doing good. They expanded to a bigger building around the corner from where we were just posted up at," Rich revealed.

"So, let's just rush in on them and do what we gotta do. I'm tired of this back and forth. I know you not trying to hear all that though."

"I told you we gone get them boyz. Please believe that. We're just gonna do it smart. We already got eyes on them clowns. Let them stack up some more. The more they stack, the more we take. Them niggas just moved into their building so let them get comfortable."

"Ok baby, you lead and I'm still following," I spoke.

"Yeah, I fuckin' love you, girl," Rich grabbed me. Pulling me closer to him before kissing me softly. "I wanna cuddle right here on this couch with you," he continued.

"I need to shower first, Rich. But after that, I'm all yours."

"I want you just like this, sweaty," Rich teased. I smiled before I began taking off my clothes.

"You like that, don't you, baby?" I asked.

Rich didn't have to respond because I could tell by the way he was licking his lips that he was enjoying it. I dropped to my knees and looked Rich in his eyes as I slid my mouth down on his thick meat, taking his entire length to the back of my throat with ease. I had his dick so far to the back of my throat I started to gag between sucks and slurps. His eyes were rolling to the back of his head, and I didn't take my eyes off of him. I could tell from the way he stared back at me and smacked my ass that he was enjoying it.

"Damn baby, this shit feels so good. Don't stop 'til you get all that nut out," Rich coached.

I straddled Rich, easing his shaft into me, riding him slowly. He moaned softly in my ear, causing me to become wetter. I could hear the sounds of my gushy with each movement.

"You like that?" I whispered. When Rich didn't answer me, I said it louder.

"I said do you like this pussy?"

"Ah yes, baby, I love it," Rich yelled out to me.

He could barely speak and the little words that he could get out were slurred. He couldn't help but to let his nut go inside me. We both were spent and laid there on the couch.

"I'm about to go take a shower," I finally spoke.

I bet he think twice before he wants to fuck another bitch. I thought to myself as I got up from the couch.

"Baby, you did your thang, damn I couldn't hold my nut

back. I wanted to feel that pussy longer, but I couldn't keep my shit in," Rich spoke.

"I can't move, you probably gotta carry me to the shower now," Rich joked.

"Stop playing, boy, let's get in this shower together."

TWENTY-ONE
LILY

It was the middle of the night when Rich got a phone call from Terrence. Mario had been rushed to the hospital for abnormal breathing and a high fever. Rich and I rushed to get dressed and drove 90 mph on the Interstate. Once we arrived at the hospital, Terrence was standing outside smoking a blunt.

"Man, what happened, son?" Rich asked him.

"That boy had a high ass fever, man. His mama hit me on my cell, and I rushed over there. That's when I saw his breathing wasn't right. Nigga said he couldn't taste or smell, I got him to the hospital as fast as I could."

"Damn bro, I hope he pushes through bruh, a lot of people not making it through." Rich said sadly. "Y'all know that COVID-19 is going around heavy, did the doctors test him?" he asked.

"Yeah, they tested him as soon as they found out he had the symptoms," Terrence responded.

"Are they letting anyone in right now?"

"No, doctors said they checked his oxygen levels and had to

hurry and put him on a ventilator. They are not letting anyone in his room due to COVID, they have been taking precautions. His mama standing in the lobby, let's walk in and see if the doctor came with any new information," Terrence spoke, as we followed him to the lobby.

"Hello, Ms. Jones, how are you?" Rich asked.

"Hello, Rich, I'm doing ok; I'm glad that you're both are here."

"It's going to be okay. Mario has the best doctor around and he's going to take care of him. Right now, all we can do is wait," his mother continued.

"This is my girlfriend, Lily. Lily, this is Mario's mother, Ms. Jones," Rich introduced us.

"Nice to meet you, Mrs. Jones," I extended my hand.

"Nice to meet you, too," she replied.

"I'll be over there waiting for you, take your time." I pointed over to a chair that was located by the window. I wanted to give Rich the space to speak about his friend in private.

"Ok baby, I'll be right over in a few," Rich told me, before turning his attention back to Ms. Jones and Terrence, just as the doctors started walking towards them.

"Ms. Jones, Mario should be ok; we just want to monitor him for a few days. We were able to get his oxygen levels back to normal. It's been dropping but it seems to be elevating as we speak. We just have to pray, and everything will be ok; he will pull through. We tested him for COVID, and the test was positive, so now we just wait and monitor him," the doctor informed.

"Thank you so much," Ms. Jones spoke.

"Why are you crying, baby?" Rich asked me. Walking over to me and finding tears in my eyes.

"Rich, baby, I know how Ms. Jones is feeling. But for it to be her son is awful. I know she has to be so scared. I pray that everything is okay and that he recovers."

"Lily, tell me what's on your mind, baby."

"My grandmother passed away from Covid while I was locked up. She already had cancer, and I knew she was sick. I just thought we would have more time. Then Covid came. When she got it, her body just couldn't fight it. I wasn't even able to say goodbye to her. My grandmother was all I had, and now she's gone. I wasn't even able to go to the funeral because I was locked up. All my life, my grandmother had been there for me through everything. And the one time she needed me, I couldn't even be there for her."

"It's ok, Lily, God had it written already. She's in good hands now. She's in a better place, she's happy, and she knows you love her."

Rich hugged me, giving me comfort in his arms. Tears rolled down my cheeks. Being in this hospital, watching Ms. Jones scared for her son's life was all too much for me. It made me realize just how much I missed my grandmother. "Rest In Peace, Sarah Lee Williams," I whispered, as the tears fell.

"Let's roll out, baby," Rich suggested, kissing me on my forehead.

When we returned home from the hospital, I went into the bathroom to wash my face. My eyes were red and puffy from all the crying I'd done, and I just wanted to relax. I truly missed my grandmother, and I wished there was a way I could turn back the hands of time. Everything was different for me now, the one person that I could call for anything was gone, and it still felt unreal. Rich left again after dropping me off, and this time I'd stayed behind.

Everything that was going on had me thinking. I wanted to do better in life, especially since I had done all of that time in prison. If I wouldn't have been in prison, I could have been there for my grandmother. I would have been able to spend her last days with her. Maybe then I wouldn't feel so heartbroken.

Rich wasn't pressuring me into doing anything, he actually had my best interest at heart. I wanted to do it all on my own to help Rich bring his cousin's killers to an end. I needed time to think about how I wanted my life to go after the revenge on Rich's cousin's killer. In the middle of thinking my phone vibrated in my lap.

"Hello," I answered.

"What's up, baby?" an unfamiliar voice spoke into the phone. The only person that called me baby was Rich, and I knew for a fact this wasn't him.

"May I ask who's speaking?" I asked politely.

"You don't know my voice? This is TT, girl. Now, greet me like you miss me."

"Hey, wow! I wasn't expecting you to call me, seeing that you didn't call me when I got out. I guess you was too busy playing with another hoe, and you couldn't find the time for me huh?"

"Wait, what? Hell naw, it wasn't even like that. I just wanted to wait until I touched down. I'm home now and I want to see you. I'm doing a turn-around trip to Atlanta, and you know what I want, I want to taste you," TT spoke bluntly.

"You just made my panties wet," I responded. "Just let me know when you land, and I will pull up."

"I'm driving out there, so it will take me sometime but I'm coming no doubt," TT informed.

"What are you coming out here for if you don't mind me asking?"

"I'm coming to cop a new whip, you know y'all ride foreign out there and they be clean."

I knew TT was lying. I felt like TT was coming out here to get some drugs. TT was locked up on drug charges, my guess was probably right. But I let her talk and didn't call her out.

"I can't wait to see you when you get here," I told TT.

"I know you can't!"

I had some time to think if I really wanted to meet TT later. My mind was quickly made up and about nine hours later, my phone rang again. It was almost 11:00 PM and Rich still hadn't made it home.

"Hello," I answered, thinking it was Rich.

"Meet me at the Holiday Inn," TT spoke, before hanging up the phone.

I looked at my phone to call TT back because there were a million Holiday Inns in Atlanta, but TT had already dropped her location. I put on some lingerie, put together an overnight bag, and headed out of the door. I still didn't know why Rich wasn't answering his phone. *Oh well, I'll be back,* I told myself.

Pulling up to the hotel I checked my phone again to make sure I had the right room number. Entering the hotel lobby in a trench coat and heels, I strutted through the lobby looking and feeling like a million bucks. Looking over to my left I saw TT smiling at one of the thirsty old men that watched me walk. TT caught me by surprise by meeting me in the lobby. She walked up to me and hugged me, as everybody stared at the lesbian action that was going on in front of them.

"What y'all laughing and staring at?" TT asked.

We both walked to the elevator doors and traveled to her floor. Before the doors could even open good, we were already tugging at each other's clothes. Once inside the room we pleased each other all night long.

TWENTY-TWO

LILY

The next morning, I rolled over in the hotel bed and TT was standing in front of me with a plate of hot breakfast. She brought me an omelet loaded with three cheeses, sausages, and bacon.

"Thank you for thinking about my stomach, it smells good," I kissed her passionately.

"Hey, that's enough with all that morning breath," she joked.

"I'm about to smash this food and shower so don't worry about that," I snapped back playfully.

I finished eating and got into the shower, and before I knew it, TT had come into the room watching me. TT couldn't get enough of me; I was her little boo thang. I didn't know how long this would last, but I liked it for the time being. TT knew I didn't belong to her, but that didn't mean we couldn't have fun from time to time. I wasn't gay or really into girls, but it was something about TT that attracted me to her.

"Oh TT," I moaned. She was finger fuckin' my juice box with two fingers and I was soaking wet.

The noise that was heard throughout the shower told TT that I was pleased, my juice box was being punished. She got down on her knees and ate me from the back. I was pressed against the wall with one leg up. TT's tongue was doing marvelous things inside of me.

"You taste so good and sweet," she roared out to me.

"This pussy is the best I've ever had," she proclaimed, smacking me on the ass.

"Awe yes, TT, you're about to make me cum."

"Cum for me then, baby."

I let go right inside of TT's mouth. I was so out of breath, but TT had that effect on me every time. Turning to TT, I dropped to my knees and gave TT the best head she had ever had.

TT was in heaven and couldn't believe I was giving her head like this. Afterwards, we both rested in each other's arms like we wouldn't see each other again.

I started getting dressed and was thinking, *Damn, I know I can't see myself with a female for the rest of my life. But that girl knows how to make me feel special mentally and physically, and if Rich messes up again, I would be in TT's arms forever.*

I met TT downstairs, standing next to her brand new all red Benz.

"I like this," I told her while getting into the car.

"Where did you get this?"

"I been had this one, I'm getting another one today hopefully. I like nice things, so I'm hoping Atlanta treats me well while car shopping today. I got this one before I went to jail, that's why it still looks brand new."

"Ok then, I wish I had it going on like you."

"It turns out I'll be out here another day, so I really would like to see you again tonight. I'll be leaving tomorrow night, and I don't know when I'll be back down here," TT spoke.

"You know Rich will start thinking crazy. He knows I don't know anyone here and I barely go anywhere. So, I'm not sure how I could make that happen. He's going to think I'm out with another man."

"He will be wrong because I'm not a man and he should appreciate me."

"I left last night without telling him where I would be, he was gone already so I just left."

"Seems to me *he's* the one who needs to be coming up with an excuse, he's out late at night and shit, no telling what he had going on. Tell him you found a home girl out here and you want to chill with her tonight."

"I will think of something to tell him, you gone get me in trouble, TT."

"If that nigga touch you and I know about it, he gone bite the dust; that's on me, shawdy. Just text me when you are ready for me to pull back up."

"Say Lily," she yelled to get my attention. "I enjoyed you last night, don't change up on me."

"You don't ever have to worry about that or question my loyalty, I've explained that to you. Don't ever doubt me. I told you that," I replied.

"I will be waiting on you to text me later tonight, I want to take you out to eat if that's fine with you," she informed before driving off.

I wasn't ready to step inside of my house to face Rich, but I had to. I already knew Rich was pissed off because my dumb ass didn't even call him, I was so caught up in TT's arms. When I entered the house after being out all night, Rich was sitting in the living room.

"You scared me, baby, why are you sitting in here like that?" I asked him.

"I've been worried about you all night; I have been up waiting for you to come home. Where were you, Lily? I called and texted you and you never responded."

"Just like how I called and texted you all night and you ignored me, what's up with that?" I asked.

"Don't play with me, Lily, you know what the fuck I be out there doing and don't answer my question with a question. You know what I be doing, I'm out getting paid, so we won't have to worry about a thing. You see all this designer shit in the closet, how do you think I was able to get all of that? If I don't go out and get it, we won't eat!" he yelled.

"I know, baby, and I appreciate you very much. I know I got someone good. What do you think was the real reason I stayed after you cheated on me? Yeah, I didn't have anywhere else to go, but it was because I love and appreciate you from the bottom of my heart. I'm not going anywhere, and I'm not out there cheating on you if that's what you are thinking."

I went ahead and used the lie TT told me to use because Rich didn't look too thrilled or convinced with what I had said so far.

"Baby, I went to the grocery store yesterday to get something to cook, and I met a friend. She seemed a little cool, so I gave her my number."

"Lily, you gave a complete stranger your phone number?" he asked in disbelief.

"Yes baby, we have so much in common; she loves to cook and so do I. That's all we talked about. She texted me last night to go with her to a kickback at her homegirl's house. It was late, and I was too drunk to drive us back. So, I crashed at her spot."

"So, you went to the store and met a complete stranger, y'all discussed cooking, but Lily, you didn't even cook, where's the food?"

"Baby, I got sidetracked and just didn't cook."

"Okay but that doesn't explain why you didn't answer my texts or calls, Lily."

"Honestly, baby, I was mad because you ignored me most of the day."

He shook his head at me. "Don't do that shit again," he ordered.

"Okay baby, well her and her homegirls are celebrating all weekend."

"Oh yea? What's the occasion?"

"One of her homegirls recently got her first book published," I lied.

"So, you're going out again tonight, Lily?"

"Yes, only if that's ok with you, baby?"

I waited for a response, hoping he wouldn't trip. Rich gave me a smile and told me don't be out all night this time.

"Come here, let me smell that pussy."

I walked over to my man with no worries. I knew I didn't smell like sex because I wasn't getting any dick. I was only getting ate out good and my finger fucked by my bitch. Later that night, TT came to pick me up and we headed back to the hotel where she was staying. I didn't want TT anywhere near my man, so I would drive myself back home tonight since my car was out front.

"It smells good in here."

I opened the door and breathed in a cloud of purp.

"I gotta make one stop before I take you out to eat," TT told me.

I laid back in my seat and bopped my head to the music. When she pulled up to a familiar area, my attention focused on what was going on around me.

"What are you doing here?" I asked.

"Oh, I'm about to cop something really quick from my little connect."

I couldn't believe I was in the same neighborhood as Rich's cousin's killers. Two men walked up to TT and gave her a brown bag. She shook their hands and got back into the car.

"How do you know them?" I immediately asked.

"Shid, who don't know them niggas? Them niggas got the best product that's out here right now. They are known throughout all the states, especially in Texas. Them niggas balling out of control. Seriously, that's the real reason I came out here."

TT finally admitted why she came out to Atlanta for real. I knew she was lying about coming to cop a whip though. TT was already riding in style, brand fuckin' new off the lot car smell.

"So, they ballin' like that? Damn, I wonder what all they be pushing."

I was talking now, probing to see what all TT knew so I could go back and tell Rich that he knew exactly what he was talking about and what he was thinking was true.

"Why, you know them or something?"

"Nope, not at all."

I smiled and took one last look at the area before TT drove off. I was ready to eat and get back to the hotel. TT was about to blow my back out and then I had to get back home to my man to give him all the good news that I came across today about the opps.

TWENTY-THREE
LILY

"**B**aby, wake up!" I called out to Rich as I rushed into our bedroom, shaking him out of his sleep.

"Stop it, Lily, I'm sleeping good," Rich told me.

"I got some shit to tell you about yo cousin's killers," I spoke, prompting Rich to sit up instantly.

"When I went out with my homegirl last night, I didn't know she smoked but she does, so we pulled up to that same building that belongs to your cousin's killer. When she got back into the car, I asked immediately if the niggas were balling because she had just copped a few things from one of them."

"What's she say?" he asked.

"Well, she said they push heavy weight throughout the states and their main stomping ground is Texas, but they are well known all over. She also told me they've been doing this for years and that they got workers everywhere."

Rich stood up and grabbed a bottled water from the mini fridge that was kept inside our bedroom.

"Let's get ready to move in on them clowns, we want the

cash and then I want their heads on chopping boards, yah dig," he responded.

Rich was with the shits early this morning, and I was all for it.

"So, here's the plan, we pull up on them clown ass niggas and wait for them to get to the warehouse. As soon as they pull the door up to go inside, we're going in with them with our guns wide open. You will wear this shit, Lily, without complaining," Rich spoke.

He handed me a black, long sleeve shirt, a black hoodie, black leggings, black Air Max, and a black ball cap. "I'll be matching you with the same shit on," he continued. I stood there smiling at the way he was handling me. His gangster side was turning me on.

I was ready to get at these niggas just as much as he was. I wanted to show him I was down for him in every way. I knew helping him get revenge on the people that killed his family would do just that. "When we ridin' out?" I asked.

"Tomorrow night, the quicker we move in the quicker we get straight. It's a lot of money involved in this shit, and it's all 'bout to be ours," he informed.

We pulled up to Tiger and Jon Jon's warehouse. I'd brought snacks because I didn't know how long we would be waiting.

"Man, I don't know why you bring all that shit with you, baby. I already know you love to eat fruit and that's why that pussy tastes so sweet when I'm eating it but damn," Rich joked.

Rich grabbed my cell phone and called Terrence to check on Mario's condition.

"Yo bro, what's the word on Mario?"

"Oh, shid, he straight, nigga pulled through. I was planning to call and give you the update tomorrow when we knew for sure that he was coming home."

"So, they talkin' bout lettin' him come home tomorrow? That's wassup."

"I spoke to Ms. Jones earlier and she told me the doctor said he would be good to leave tomorrow morning," Terrence announced.

"That's good news, bro, tell that nigga don't scare us like that again. But look bro, we are at the spot; I will let you know what the deal is once it's a done deal."

"Say less bro, just hit me up later," Terrance spoke before they ended the call.

I looked at my phone to get the time. It had been two hours over the time they were supposed to get here, they always arrived at the same time every night. Rich have been clocking their every move every day. Before I could finish my thought, a car pulled up. Rich observed the whip, trying to see who the car belonged to. He'd never seen it before in all the times he'd watch the house, so he was unsure who it was. The spaceship-looking Corvette sat there and moments later, Tiger pulled in. So much shit was going on around us, we couldn't risk blowing our cover, so we drove the fuck off.

TWENTY-FOUR
LILY

"Who the hell was that?" I asked as soon as we walked into the house.

"Man, I don't know. That's why we had to get the hell outta there. We gotta make sure to get them at the right time so we can come out on top," Rich stated.

"Yeah, I agree. That was crazy, this calls for some wine."

"Fuckin' right, but fuck the wine, get me a shot of henny."

"Baby, what spooked me was that they arrived late and the different vehicle that pulled up. I ain't never seen that vehicle before and we couldn't take that chance," Rich continued.

"Better safe than sorry because shit could have gotten real out there. How we know they weren't on to us? So shid, leaving like we did was the best decision," I told him.

"Let's just enjoy this wine and shots and regroup."

"Baby, what you think was going on though?"

"I don't know but we are not going to stop here, we are just going to move smarter. In this game there are no fuck ups, Lily."

"I'm about to step out and make a few calls, I'll be back inside in a few."

"Okay, I will be right here waiting," I replied.

When Rich stepped outside, I decided to cook a meal for the both of us. A nice healthy meal because your girl was trying to watch her weight and Rich needed to stay healthy. I decided to grill steaks, with a side of vegetables. My man was crazy about steak but I did not know how he was gonna feel about the side of vegetables. *I'm going to make them extra tasty for him. It's late but we still gotta eat.*

Rich stepped back inside of the house after an hour and a half on the phone, which gave me plenty of time to prepare our meal. From the look on his face, he didn't look so happy, he looked pissed off.

"Baby, are you ok?" I asked him.

"Yeah, I'm good, I'm straight; just had to make a phone call… I'm good though, everything's straight."

I knew my man way too well to know that everything wasn't ok. Deep down, I knew something was wrong because he kept saying he was good. Normally when he said he was good and kept repeating himself, he wasn't good.

"Alright well, I made us steak and vegetables!"

"Sounds cool, but don't put no vegetables on my plate," Rich told me nonchalantly.

"No vegetables? But vegetables are very healthy for you; you need to eat some vegetables," I begged him playfully.

"Nah, I'm good on the vegetables, just give me two steaks."

"How about I give you one steak, and after you eat it, I'll let you eat some vegetables off of me, would that make it better?"

"Oh, hell yeah, now you are talking… shit, let me go ahead and eat this steak right quick so I can take you all the way down through there."

What a damn good night we had! I said to myself as I woke up with my man lying next to me. From the way that he was snoring, I knew he would agree. I decided to get up and shower before Rich woke up and I also felt like making him a nice hot meal to get our day started. While I was walking into the bathroom, I checked my phone to see that I had 68 missed calls from TT. Why was she blowing me up like this? She knew what my situation was. She couldn't be doing this, she was gonna get me caught the fuck up.

This shit had to come to an end but the lovin' was so good. TT made this shit feel so right, but I knew it was wrong. She took damn good care of my body sexually and I felt so good. I peeped outside of the door to make sure that Rich was still sound asleep and of course he still was, so I hurried up and dialed her number.

"Yo, why you haven't been answering none of my phone calls?" TT asked, picking up on the first ring.

"Yo, why you gotta answer the phone like that? You are so fuckin' rude. When you see my name pop up on the caller ID, you address me as your queen," I said with a laugh. I didn't understand why TT was trippin'. She knew I had a man. So, if I didn't answer, that meant I was with him. What I didn't understand was why she would call so many times after I didn't answer the first time.

"You can't sneak out for nothing to answer my phone call? What, you were too busy taking that nigga's dick? You couldn't even answer my call. You know what it is, keep acting dumb."

"Listen, TT, if you can't respect my situation and what I got going on, what we have going on has to end."

And just like that, I regretted the words that had just rolled off of my tongue because I knew TT was about to cut the fuck up.

"What the fuck you mean, *this gotta end*? Man, this will **never** end. If you even think about letting this shit end, you already know what comes next. If you not with me, I guess you won't be with nobody."

"TT, are you threatening me now?" I asked, confused.

"Fuck no, I'm *promising* you now, you know how I'm coming."

"Wait a minute now! I'm seeing a whole different side of you. You are not the same TT that I met when we were incarcerated."

"Yeah, well people change, and situation changes especially when you're involved with someone that you have caught feelings for. So, don't fuck with me," TT spoke firmly.

"Oh, so now you got feelings for a bitch?"

"I been caught feelings for you, can't you see how I came all way out here for you?"

"No, you came out here for other things but that's another story."

"I came out here for *you*. That other shit was just a bonus."

"Don't try to sell me on that bullshit and have me feeling all jittery inside."

"Man, I ain't playing games with you and you heard what I said. Don't you ever fix your mouth to tell me about no shit like that again. This shit will never end with us."

"Look, whatever, now what did you kept calling me for?"

"You already know, I want to see yo' fine ass."

"See me?" I asked.

"Same location tonight, you gonna pull up? Wait, know what, scratch that, it will be a different location tonight. I'll drop you the address in a minute."

"Wait, what are you changing the location for?" I asked, confused.

"I'm changing locations, why you got a problem with that?"

"No problem. I'm just saying it's easier and faster for me to get to the same place we always meet at. Stop changing things up!"

"Look, ma, I'm gonna drop you the address, pull up because I got a pool party happening at my spot."

"Your spot? You moved out here or something?"

"Nah, I just got a spot for us to go, that's all. Calm down, you don't have to panic."

"Okay, drop me the address and I'll be there."

"Alright, and Lily, wear some something sexy for me."

"Yeah, a sexy ass bathing suit just for you. What do you want them to be? Edible, so that you can eat them off of me."

"Fuckin' right, edible sounds delicious to me! See you tonight and I bet next time you better not take too damn long answering my calls or calling me back."

I knew I had to been on that phone damn nearly 30 minutes feeding into TT's bullshit. I brushed my teeth and hurried up and took a shower, hoping to make it out before Rich woke up, because I knew he would be hungry.

After getting myself together, I stepped out of the bathroom and my man was still asleep. I hurried into the kitchen and made a quick meal, making eggs, bacon, a muffin, and orange juice on the side. I prepared my man's plate just like they do on the TV. I walked back into the room and to his bedside, waking him up with the aroma of a freshly cooked breakfast. I looked at him like I had been up cooking and cleaning all morning, knowing damn well my ass been up to no good.

"Sit up and eat, baby," I smiled.

TWENTY-FIVE
LILY

Later that evening Rich left to go hit a few licks. I didn't really too much worry about Rich when he was out in those streets by himself because he knew how to take care of himself. He knew to watch his back. I wasn't worried about other bitches either, they didn't intimidate me anymore. Rich knew what he had at home waiting for him. Besides, Rich also knew that I was crazy, and I would fuck him up and that bitch up if I found out he was cheating on me again.

I really didn't have room to talk because of the things that I was doing. Although it was not with a guy, I was still cheating. Cheating was cheating, but I couldn't think about all of that right now, maybe another time. Right now, I had some spare time to get myself together the right way because Rich wouldn't be back until later.

I grabbed the bathing suit from the closet, one that I hadn't worn before, it wasn't edible, but TT would be okay. I wasn't planning to wear any pants or anything under the silky purple button up long sleeve that I chose to wear over it. Rich knew that I was going to a pool party, so my attire didn't matter. I threw some flip flops on my feet; my pedicured toes looked good enough to eat. I took a couple shots, glanced at my phone to see that TT had already dropped her location, and looked back in the mirror one last time. I didn't care that it was already dark outside, I still put my shades on, grabbed my keys, and headed out of the door.

The shots that I had taken had already kicked in and I had to catch myself because I was going 85 in a 60 mile per hour zone. I surely didn't want to get pulled over by the police because I wouldn't have any words to explain why I was speeding and tipsy. The GPS was taking me all the way around the world, it kept rerouting me because a lot of roads were closed, but I finally made it. Pulling up to a nice upscale neighborhood just right outside of Columbus, GA, TT had me way out here, but it was surely nice. Looked like a lot of rich folks stayed in the area. I didn't have to waste any time calling TT to let her know that I was outside because she was standing right in the door, waiting for me to get out of the car. Instead of her coming to open my door she just stood by the front door and let me open my door myself. *She is so rude*, I said to myself.

"What's up, man? I see you made it," TT said to me as I approached the front door.

"Yeah, yeah, I'm here so let's go inside."

I went inside, there were a lot of activities going on. The house was huge and nicely decorated. I didn't know if TT was renting it or buying it, let her tell it, she'd never tell the truth. They had the spades game going, she had a room for playing pool, and just around the corner from the pool room, there was an inside pool. I wasted no time heading towards the pool but TT stopped me.

"Hey ma, where you are going?" she asked me.

"Oh, I'm going to jump in the pool."

"Just like that, you don't want to sit and talk to me for a minute?"

"No, what's there to talk about? You invited me here to talk? I thought we were here to have some fun," I joked.

"Come on… follow me over to the bar."

We got to the bar, and I had a seat on the stool. I couldn't believe my eyes, I seen two lines of coke staring back at me.

"Go ahead," TT offered me a line of ATL's finest snow.

I didn't wanna snort a line of coke, but it was right in front of me. I was really trying to do better, but I couldn't help myself. I was a pro at this shit and in one sniff, it was gone. I went to sniff the second line but was stopped.

"Damn man, that was fast, the fuck?"

"I'm sorry, TT, but you know this is my drug of choice and I try my best to stay away from it."

"Oh, I'm not trying to be a bad influence on you. A nigga ain't trying to get you to do nothing you do not want to do. If this makes you feel uncomfortable, we can stop right now."

"I'm good TT, I want to do it, you're not making me."

TT then snorted her line, but she did hers a little slower than me.

"Damn TT, this some good shit, shit got my whole world spinning." I could hear myself slurring as I said that. The room was starting to spin faster and faster and faster and everything around me sounded numb.

"TT give me more," I whispered.

"I ain't got no more right now, ma, but I got some more

coming later. Let's just go chill over by the pool until it gets here."

We both walked to the pool, and I jumped in first. TT jumped in the pool next to me, we relaxed, and we talked. There were so many people in the party and TT was playing with them hoes right in my face, but I was in my zone and really didn't give a fuck. I was there only to have a little fun and I was so glad everyone was starting to clear out of the pool. But I stayed in, yes, I was enjoying the feel of the water. I was so high, it felt like I couldn't come down, at least not any time soon.

TT snuck up behind me, her hands even felt numb to my body. But the feel of her tongue on my neck felt so damn good, I let her do all the freaky shit she wanted to do to me. She was kissing my neck so good and pulling my hair with the motion. She started caressing my breasts and slowly massaging my ass cheeks. I knew she was trying to fuck me right in the pool. TT had her fingers in my ass, fuckin' it something terribly, and my pussy was getting soak and wet. I couldn't help but to want what she was trying to offer me.

Without saying anything, I grabbed her hand and pulled her over to the edge of the pool. I looked back at her and instructed her to fuck me so hard. And without hesitation, she slid that 9-inch strap-on inside my tight wet pussy and did exactly what I wanted her to do. This hoe had the nerve to spit in my damn mouth. I didn't know what had come over her, but my man didn't even spit in my mouth. That shit was nasty but also turned my freaky ass up to the max. I started throwing my ass back faster, causing me to explode, and TT felt that shit. I opened my eyes from the explosion and saw that she was already putting her clothes on in a rush.

"What's going on, baby? Why are you moving so fast?" I asked in my nicest tone.

"My guy here, I gotta go grab that snow right quick."

"Well, I'm coming, so don't leave me, I gotta put a towel around myself."

"Come on then."

I went as fast as I could and followed TT, anticipating another high. I hoped it was the same shit because the shit she gave me earlier was good as fuck, I was higher than I had ever been before. I was still stumbling and walking like a damn zombie, and I was sweating too hard for someone who had just got out of the pool. TT walked ahead of me and went out of the front door while I stood and rested on the side. While TT was outside talking to a group of people, I peeped out of the window. I was so fuckin' high that my eyes had started playing tricks on me. I thought I had seen Baby Girl. *I know damn well that's not Baby Girl,* I said to myself.

I wiped my eyes for about thirty seconds and looked again as the car drove off. I gotta stop snorting that shit if it's going to have me trippin' like this. After the car full of people left, TT walked back inside talking that shit.

"You ready for some more of this shit, ma?" TT asked.

"Which one? I liked them both," I joked.

"You can't have any more of this good meat right now, but bring your ass on here so we can do another line."

"Hell yeah!"

We ran back over to the bar; I sat in the same spot on the stool again. I snorted my line faster this time, and TT snorted hers slowly again. I looked at TT and I was seeing triple of her now.

"Baby, I'm ready to fuck again," I told TT.

TWENTY-SIX

LILY

When I made it home it was late as fuck. Rich had told me he wasn't going to be mad, but I knew he would be. It was almost four in the morning and I was just walking through the door. Rich went out and did his thing, but I knew he felt like that was different because he was a man.

"Baby, I thought you would be home hours ago. What's up with that?" Rich asked.

"Come on, baby, I told you I was going to a pool party. I was having fun and lost track of time. I know you have lost track of time before," I replied.

"Yeah baby, but it's four in the morning. What kind of pool party lasts this long? I don't like this shit, Lily," Rich said honestly.

"You don't like what?"

"You being out like this. We got way too much going on for you to be out in the streets."

"So, you don't want me to hang out anymore?" I asked, confused.

"Not if you gon' stay out this late."

I rolled my eyes before telling him we would talk in the morning. I was high and sleepy. All I wanted to do was lay in my bed and close my eyes. Anything Rich had to say about me going out could wait until I woke up. It was late in the evening when I finally woke up and to my surprise, Rich had cooked for me. He didn't even wake me up, he let me sleep the whole time.

I slept 10 hours straight without being waken up. At first, I was kind of mad because he knew I liked to do things throughout the day; but when I woke up to the smell of yams, lamb chops, and cornbread I wasn't even mad no more. My man had gotten in the kitchen and did his thing, he knew not to even bring me wine because I had already been out all night and had a little hangover. He brought me water and dinner to my bedside.

"Baby, are you going to stay and eat with me?"

"Uh-huh."

Rich left out of the room and went back into the front. I guess he had some business to go handle because he didn't sit in the room and eat with me. I got to thinking about last night, I just know my eyes weren't playing tricks on me. I still couldn't remember if that was Baby Girl that I saw or was I just that delusional. I couldn't be, I really wanna ask TT who that girl was that came to the spot last night to drop off the package. It was about four bitches out there unless I just got her to name all of them because I really wanna know what's going on. And was one of them named Cameron AKA Baby Girl.

While I was incarcerated, I did hear something about her allegedly living in Georgia. I didn't know what part of Georgia, but I didn't move to Georgia to find Baby Girl, I would run across her in due time. But if that was her, why was she over there delivering work? That shit had me kind of puzzled. I was so high last night I couldn't even think straight. If I would have known it was her for sure, she would have been fucked up.

I would have beaten her ass on site and probably killed her out there. So, I had to do a little bit more investigating cause I didn't want no fuck ups when it came to Cameron Jackson. I looked at my phone and there were no text messages and there were no missed calls so I was guessing that TT must have gotten the picture, if I don't call you first, don't text or call me first. At least I hoped she had gotten the picture cause I was so sick of all the random approaches.

Rich walked back into the room about 15 minutes later.

"Hey baby, are you okay?"

"Yeah, I'm straight, how was your night?"

"I had a good night, it was okay. I just hung out with some friends at the little pool party, good vibes."

"Good vibes huh?"

"Yeah, good vibes."

"Oh yeah, what all you do out there?"

"Oh nothing, nothing spectacular; we just played pool and got into an indoor pool. A little cute and elegant event."

"I like elegant… next time, won't you invite me with you."

"Okay, that's cool, baby; you can go with me," I lied.

"You were being good out there though huh, weren't no men out there?"

"Of course, I was being good and no men except for the girls' boyfriends and husbands. It wasn't a gathering like that. I was there with my homegirl and that was it."

"Let me ask you something, can I trust you?"

"Of course, baby, where is all this coming from? See, we were doing so good; everything was going so well, don't start no shit."

"I'm just asking, you know just asking can I trust you because you can trust me. With everything we've been through, I learned my lesson, just don't try to get back on me because it ain't gonna end well."

"Oh no, I'll never do that… I forgave you, remember?"

"Yeah, you forgave me, but you said you would never *forget*."

"Yeah, I said that, but you know time does heal, I've gotten over it."

"Yeah, I bet you have. Let me tell you something, Lily, I'm looking straight into your eyes as I tell you this… ***Don't fuck over me cause if you fuck over me, I gotta fuck over you and I'm not talking about cheating. I will turn up around this bitch.*** Do you want that?"

"No Rich, baby, I'm not doing anything though," I lied.

"Alright, keep it that way, don't let me find out you lying to me or it will not turn out good for you."

"Look, let's just finish eating and have some alone time; just us talking, hugging, kissing, watching movies, and just loving each other. You down with that?"

"Yeah, I've been down with it, you just make sure you down with it and *only* that."

"Okay babe, but you're acting weird all of a sudden."

"No, I'm not acting weird; I'm being serious… don't take me as a joke and get took down through there. I love you, girl!"

"I love you more, baby."

And just like that, Lily had lied to my face, Rich mused to himself.

"Baby, we need to start back discussing how we're going to

get Tiger and Jon Jon. Shid, you may have stopped talking about it, but I have still been thinking about it heavily. We already know the spot, we just gotta find the right time to move in on them clowns. I'm not letting them clowns get away with what they did, that's not an option." Rich spoke.

"So, let's roll up on them tonight."

"You see how they have been moving lately? They've been moving kinda funny, it's like they know somebody watching or some. I don't wanna get into deep thought with that though… I don't wanna feel like they know somebody watching them even if it's not me that they know. I ain't trying to move like that and get myself killed."

"Yeah, I understand, baby, and I'm with you a hundred percent. I was gonna ask you if I can go out tonight."

"Really Lily, again, tonight? I just told you what I need you to do with me, and in the same conversation, you ask me that bullshit."

"Yeah, I mean after we get done handling that business, I was just trying to see if it was ok for me to go hang out."

"You've been hanging out a lot lately, I'm sort of thinking you on some bullshit. Don't be fuckin' over me behind my back, like I told you earlier, don't let me find out."

"Don't be silly. Come on now, you know I ain't rocking like that."

"I don't know what to think no more."

"What you mean by that?"

"Don't worry about it."

"I tell you what, Lily, you gone and go out with your little friends and you have fun. This a man's job anyways, I don't need you rolling with me. Not right now anyways, if I need you, I'll let you know," Rich spoke.

"Come on, baby, don't be like that. You know I wanna have your back."

"Girl what? I can't tell."

"Don't make me feel like that. Don't make me feel like I ain't trying to ride with you and you know I got your back, baby."

"Yeah, well lately, you've been acting a little funny and I can't really tell, but for real though, I got this part. I'm gonna need you later on, you go out and have some fun. What time are you leaving anyway?"

"I am leaving about ten."

"Oh, okay and what time will you be back? Don't let it be too late this time. I don't want to have to roll up on you and drag you out by your neck, Lily."

"Oh no, I won't be out too late." *You won't even know where I am at to drag me out by my neck,* Lily thought to herself evilly.

"Yeah, alright."

<hr>

"Man, what the fuck you got on, Lily?" Rich called out when I walked into the room hours later.

"It's my outfit for tonight, you like it, daddy?"

"Oh, hell no, I don't like it. Why you got this shit on? You not single, only single bitches and hoes dress like that."

"What do you mean? It's some shorts and a short shirt."

"Some little ass shorts and a little ass shirt. That's not a fuckin' shirt anyways, that's a damn bra. You call that a shirt, then I really know that you are either sick in the head or really don't give a damn."

"Don't be like that, you know that I'm only for you."

"The way that you are dressed looks like you for everybody.

I don't want my girl out there like that; dressed to impress them clowns because you should be at home impressing me."

"But I'm not looking for no one else, I'm going to hang out with my friends."

"Where are you going to hang out at, Lily?"

"We are going to a lil' pool hall," I replied, not telling him which one.

"Yeah, a pool hall full of niggas. Like I said, why you wanna be trifling? But go ahead, take yo' trifling ass on." Rich responded.

"Why are you talking to me like that? You know I'm not even that type of girl."

"I don't know what you are anymore because you done changed on me… now it's like I'm sharing you with somebody else."

"Why would you think that?"

"It ain't what I *think*, it's how I've been feeling and it's how you been moving."

"Well, I'm not messing around with nobody else, so is it cool if I wear this tonight?"

"I told you go ahead and wear it, I ain't tripping."

Deep down, I know lately I'd been tripping; I'd been with TT, and I'd been with my man too. I know that shit ain't right. This was a dangerous game that I was playing. I know I had to get it right. I was going out this last time, I know I kept saying it but I was serious this time.

I gotta get right, I gotta get right for my man because he loved me. He deserved for me to be the woman that he made, the vulnerable woman that he made. So, I was going to do the right thing, tonight was my last night going out with TT. I gotta tell her, I gotta tell her this time and be serious. Lily thought for a second before responding back to Rich with tears running down her face.

"OK baby, I love you and I will see you in a few hours."

Lily knew she was out there doing me dirty that's why her ass was crying.

"Love you too."

TWENTY-SEVEN
LILY

Normally, TT would have met me at the corner. However, for some reason, she wasn't able to make it tonight to pick me up. So, I convinced Rich to let me drive one of his cars, so without hesitation, Rich complied. While I was walking out of the house and damn near to the curb where the car was parked, I realized I had left my clutch. As I was about to trod back into the house, I saw a dark colored car with dark windows pull up to the curb and started shooting out of nowhere.

I didn't know what was going on, and I had no idea what was happening. I didn't even know anyone that had a car that looked like that. It was crazy. I started running, trying to find a safe spot to duck at. But we lived out in the opening, so I had to think fast. I had no choice but to jump in the bushes and pray that no one walked up there to draw down on me. This was the life of agreeing to be a down ass bitch. I knew what I had signed up for, but how the fuck did anyone know where we lived? I never told anyone where we lived.

I laid there panicking because I didn't know what would happen next. After about a minute the shooting had stopped, and I peeped out of the bushes. I still could see the dark colored vehicle down the road. Two masked men jumped out of the car and ran towards my house. Oh, my goodness! I was panicking, I just knew they saw me jump into the bushes. I laid there for about another minute and the shooting started again then it stopped.

I laid there for another minute before peeping out of the bushes and to my surprise, I saw Rich standing there with the AK in his hand. The way that he was standing with that big ol' gun in his hand, I just knew he had just finished handling business. I saw two guys laid out on our lawn with their masks off because Rich had already revealed them. What I liked about our neighborhood was that everyone minded their own business, so no cops were called, and I rushed over to Rich.

"Baby, are you ok?" I asked Rich.

"Yeah, I'm good."

"Are you ok?"

"Yes, I'm ok, what happened? Who is this?"

I just stared at the two bodies that were laying before him.

"That's Jon Jon and that's Tiger," Rich pointed to each body.

"Wait, hold up! How the fuck did they know where we live, and how they know to come for you?"

"Honestly, I don't know and don't give two fucks. All I know is that they got what they were looking for and I got what I was looking for, too. Their mission went from war to being completed by me real quick. If anything, I want to get the other ones that pulled up with them. Did you get a look at their faces?"

"No baby, the windows were all blacked out and the license

plate was too far away for me to see. I'm surprised you're not concerned about how they found out where we lived."

"Yeah, I am, but I already told you what was important for me to find out about. Right now, this calls for a celebration, forget how these clowns got the drop on me. I will worry about that shit later. Trust me, I'm gonna do my own investigation."

I knew Rich was excited about getting Tiger and Jon Jon, but I was still worried about our location. Shit just didn't add up. I was sweaty, and I really didn't feel like attending the pool hall tonight, but I went anyway. After all this drama that went down tonight, I still wanted to hit the streets instead of going inside to be with my man. Not only that, but I could also be home trying to figure out a way to cover up the bullet holes that our home had received. None of those thoughts phased me. I went back into the house and grabbed my clutch and left my man by himself to celebrate what he'd been waiting to handle for a long time. I felt like shit.

A million thoughts were going through my head, the main thought was, how did anyone know where we lived? That was the only question I needed answers to. I never told Rich that the last time we pulled up to the warehouse where Jon Jon and Tiger were supposed to be at, a lot of weird things were happening, so we decided to leave. That same day I felt like I saw Baby Girl sitting on the passenger side, but I wasn't sure. I waited because I felt like Rich was trying to set me up, but I would be one step ahead of him.

Just the other day, I was so drunk and high, I couldn't even remember if that was Baby Girl or not at TT's house. My mind was playing tricks on me, I knew I was crazy. It's clearly safe to say that I'm delusional, too. Even though I had just finished fighting for my life, I still managed to walk up into the pool hall and meet up with TT. I was so on point, TT recognized me from the other side of the room.

I could see her hand in the air motioning for me to join her at the pool table. I rushed through the crowd and of course, a lot of niggas were trying to holla at me, but I turned them down because the only one that I wanted in the room was TT, sad to say. As soon as I made my way over to her, she wasted no time giving me a clear small bag of white powder. I held it with a closed fist and rushed to the ladies room. There were so many people fixing their makeup and fixing their hair that I couldn't even use the countertop. At that point I didn't give a damn. I ran into the bathroom stall and sat backwards on the toilet seat after putting paper down. I used the top of the toilet to spread my dope on it.

Sitting on the toilet I remembered that I didn't have anything to snort my shit with. I looked around the bathroom stall nervously because I wanted it so bad. Spotting a whole roll of tissue, I took it off the roll and rolled up a piece of the toilet paper holder to snort my line. In one big snort, that shit had vanished. The shit that TT had been passing out had me all the way fucked up and I believed that's one of the reasons why I was holding on to her cause where else would I get good shit. About ten minutes later I found myself wobbling back inside to meet TT.

"Damn baby, you alright?"

"Yeah, I'm good. You know how I get when you give me that good shit."

"Yeah, I know huh. Shid, you didn't even call me this time when you was on your way, wassup with that?"

"Yeah, I wanted to just pop up on you to make sure that you didn't have no bitches in your lap."

"Oh, you got jokes huh?"

"I'm not joking, do you see a smile on my face?"

"Yeah, there's that white girl talking, time for you to sit down. You wanna drink?"

"Yeah, I want whatever you are drinking."

"The crew on that Boosie juice tonight."

"Well, that's what I'm on too."

Minutes later, there were so many females surrounding the table. They all looked different in a variety of shapes and sizes. We were having so much fun getting so fucked up that we didn't even give a fuck. I was touching big asses and flat asses. I even touched some asses that the hoes spent all that money on for it to be hard and almost on flat. Some of them hoes looked like men, I had to be careful especially if I was planning for TT and me to leave with one of them. There was one girl who whispered in my ear and asked me if she could take me home with her.

I guess I wasn't that fucked up because I brushed that question off, but it was this one fine fem in there that I couldn't resist.

I took out my phone and texted TT even though she was sitting right beside me. I asked her did she wanna go fuck this bitch. She looked at me strangely like she couldn't believe that I was trying to engage in such activities before texting back, *hell yeah*. I motioned for the pretty bitch to come sit on my lap and she came with no hesitation.

"You wanna fuck?" I asked her, getting straight to the point.

She looked at me like, *I know she just didn't ask me no shit like that*, but she never opened her mouth to say what she really wanted to say. She stared at me for a minute, stood up, and looked at me, then glanced behind me. I guess she was trying to check and see if I was bad enough because she sure as hell was.

She said two words to me, "Let's go."

"Can my friend join us too?"

"Who is your friend?"

I pointed at TT.

"Do she carry a strap?"

"Yeah, she carries two, if you know what I mean."

"I'm gamed."

All three of us got up and left the pool hall to enjoy some alone time. When we made it to TT's car, the freaky bitch started taking off all her clothes. I ain't gone lie, them chocolate nipples looked delicious. But I couldn't give her the business in the backseat of TT's car. I changed my mind about sitting next to her in the back seat because I would be back there doing some freaky things before the show even started. I knew it was best if I went ahead and jumped in the front seat with TT. I wanted us all to be comfortable and I also wanted TT to get in on all the action and not miss a scene since she was the driver.

It took TT fifteen minutes to get across town, and we pulled up to our favorite hotel before exiting the car. We sat inside to snort some lines and take some shots. I had to tell the freaky bitch again to slow down because she was trying to get busy on site. I could tell she was freaky and getting impatient, I was getting a kick out of how bad she wanted her cookie scratched. I knew TT was too, because me and her were on the same level when it came to nasty shit.

TT

We were sitting in the car, getting high, when my phone rang. Man, who the fuck this is calling me, fuckin' up the rotation?

"Yo, who this is?"

"Say man, where you at?"

"Oh, I left a little early, I had to come take care of some business."

"Nah fam, you shouldn't have done that."

"Why you say that, my nigga?"

"The whole fuckin' pool hall just got shot up."

"What that shit got to do with me though, bro?"

"Man, son, Pop got hit."

"Man what? Don't tell me that! Man, what hospital he at?"

"Wasn't no need for the hospital man, Pop got hit in the head, bro... he gone, man."

"Man fuck! I can't believe this shit, bro."

"Everybody looking for you, TT."

"I'm way on the other side of town, fam, this shit so fucked up. Ain't no word on who did it?"

"Naw because Pop was outside talking to this little bitch, next thing you know bullets started flying. I thought you was out there with him because we didn't see you nowhere inside and I tried calling your phone, but it was going straight to voicemail."

"Yeah man, prolly because I didn't have no signal leaving that side of town. The shit must have happened as soon as I dipped out."

"Man, fuck, bro. I'll call around tomorrow and see if I can get any word on who did this shit."

"Yeah, you do that and let me know."

"Damn, I sholl hate I wasn't there."

"It's all good, it wasn't your fault, shit just happened. It wouldn't have been much you could do anyway. It hurt me to see my nigga stretched out like that, he had his gun in his waistline. He must didn't have enough time to bring that bitch out, because I know my nigga would have got to dumping if he could."

"Yeah man, all we can do now is try to get revenge on them niggas who did it and for show find out what his family need, especially his little sister."

"Alright fam, I'm about to get off the phone and go take care of this business. I can't believe I was distracted like that, bro."

"Like I told you, it's all good… it wasn't your fault."

"I already know man, I'm about to go relieve some stress, I got chills, fam."

"Aight, bet, hit me tomorrow."

"You know TT, for somebody that's not from down here, you sure do know a lot of people and then you on the phone acting like you're just a whole nigga," Lily said, trying to be playfully.

"Man, I told you I'm everywhere and I liked it down here better. Why, you got a problem with me being down here?"

"I told you I don't got no problem with you being down here. I just want to know how you be knowing all these people and you just got down here?"

"I knew people before I got here. Lily, man, I'm just not in the mood right now, one of my podnuhs just got smoked."

"Damn, I'm sorry to hear that."

"Yeah, I'm sorry to hear that too." The freaky bitch stepped up and showed me some sympathy that was real, and she didn't even know me.

"I just want to go in here and chill and have a little fun if that's ok with y'all."

"I'm cool with that."

Lily and me both looked in the back seat at the freaky bitch, we didn't even know her name, she was cool with it too.

I tried not to blow my cover because I knew who and knew why that nigga Pop got smoked. That nigga wasn't my dog, he was stealing from little old me. When I let him come to my crib the other night, I saw him on camera upstairs in my room looking through my jewelry and taking a Rolex, if he needed something, he could have just asked me. I didn't confront him about it because I knew he would lie. I had him on camera and that was all the proof I needed to show me that I was around a non-loyal ass nigga.

I hired some goons to catch the nigga outside. He got caught slipping because I had already warned them niggas that he was a true stepper, a real shooter, and he was going to bust back and wasn't going down without a fight.

TWENTY-EIGHT

RICH

ere I was sitting at home by myself like a damn duck, I couldn't believe Lily chose the streets instead of me. Out of everything we'd been through, she had changed my player's ways and now she wanna switch up on me. This shit was fucked up on so many levels. The night was still young, so I was laid back smoking blunt after blunt and taking shot after shot. I was at home by myself and stressing myself out when I could be laid up in my bitch right now. I knew my bitch was out cheating on me. She'd been in the same location for damn near four hours. There wasn't that much playing pool in the world, *playing pool my ass.*

I knew they been shut that bitch down because it was breaking news earlier about somebody getting murdered there, so I knew what she did. She left the fuckin' car at the pool hall and left with someone else. It was taking everything in me not to go after her, but as I continued to drink and smoke, my vision was getting blurry, and my mind was getting cloudy. I gotta go see what's really good with Lily and why she had been acting so strange lately. All this time she been gone, I could have easily slipped a bitch up into this house, but out of respect for my girl, I was keeping it solid until I saw otherwise.

I picked up my Glock off the table and headed for the door. I rolled up to the pool hall that I knew she was at, since she didn't wanna tell me which pool hall. She must had forgotten that I was a street nigga and knew which one she would choose even if I didn't have that tracker on the car. There was one for the older crowd and one for the younger crowd. She liked them ratchet crowds so I knew which one she would be at. Pulling into the parking lot and just like I knew it would be, her car was sitting in the parking lot along with another car. It was only two vehicles out in the parking lot, since the building had yellow tape around it. But where the fuck was Lily?

I knew how the game went. Playa ass niggas move the same way. I used to be a player. I would pick a hotel or a homeboy's house that's across town, not in the same area as where I was supposed to be at. Me knowing Lily, she was not going to no other nigga's house to fuck on nobody because she knew I knew everybody, she wouldn't take that chance. I drove across town and drove along the busy strip where all the hotels were at. There were too many of them for me to be able to find Lily, but at least I tried. I rolled around that block about fifteen times, hoping to see her walking out with a nigga. I was gonna kill them both where they stood at. Instead, I chose to just call her phone and plea with her to bring her nasty ass home, reminding her not to be out late anyways.

Her phone rang one time. I heard her pick up the phone, but nobody said anything. I knew Lily's moans from anywhere, they were damn sure pleasurable moans. Somebody was fuckin' the shit out of Lily, maxin' her ass out. Then I heard another bitch's voice that wasn't Lily. *What the fuck Lily got going on?* This nasty bitch was having a whole threesome with another nigga? Somebody else's man probably. I should have known this trick couldn't be trusted. Whoever the nigga was, he was doing his thang. I could hear the slappin' noises like he was slappin' somebody's ass cheeks. I couldn't take it anymore. Hanging up the phone, I rushed back over to the pool hall where I knew Lily would soon have to come back to because the vehicle was there.

It took me ten minutes to get back over to the pool hall, and I parked far in the back, behind a big tree. Not wanting her to see me when she pulled in. The bitch didn't even call me back, it was now almost two in the morning when a BMW came rolling up in the parking lot. I immediately put my Glock in my hand and put one in the chamber. I was getting that bitch ready for what was about to go down. First, a bitch that I didn't recognize jumped out of the car and rushed over to her dusty ass whip. Lily was still sitting in the car, so this nigga had to be somebody that Lily was fuckin' with and brought the girl along for some hoe shit.

I waited for about five more minutes and that's when I saw Lily open her door. The nigga didn't even have the manners to go around and open her door, this shit was too funny. I opened my door and shut it lightly. I was still so drunk and high, I could barely stand up straight. When the driver's side door finally opened, he stepped out the car. *Man, what the fuck? That's a damn female.* I thought to myself. Lily been playing on me with a dyke? I couldn't believe this shit; my eyes were really playing tricks on me. Man, that's a female who wanna be a nigga. This some shit that got me more heated, like I wasn't doing my job right. I immediately ran over to the car and got to bussin'. **POP. POP. POP.**

TWENTY-NINE
LILY

"No fuckin' way, do something! Oh my God! Someone help! Please call 911. I'm doing CPR," I yelled.

"I need help, I need help! TT, do *something*! Why you just fuckin' standing there? Do something please, do something, shit."

"That nigga ran upon me. He knew he wasn't ready for no gangsta shit, that nigga knew what could happen if he played with guns and can't shoot. He wasn't even a shooter, Lily. You be fuckin' wit' some ol' square ass niggas."

"Oh my gosh, how can you be so heartless?"

"Damn, Lily, you done went from hard to soft really quick. You soft for this clown. How I'm being heartless tho? He tried to kill me, and it's all because of *you*."

"How is it because of me?"

"Because it is, you shouldn't have been out here hoeing… you shouldn't have been out this time of morning with your legs open and letting me hit that ass from the back."

"You are really buggin', TT. How and why can you be like this at a time like this?"

"Check this out, I'm about to bounce because I know by now, the police have been called… you can stay here with this clown ass nigga if you want to but don't mention my name."

I couldn't believe TT was acting like this, knowing that this was all a misunderstanding. I just lost my man tonight because of some bullshit that I was doing, and that shit hurt like hell. TT had got to be out of her mind if she thought for one second that I was going to be with her or any other time after tonight. She got me fucked up; I should have stayed my ass at home. The shooting at my crib was my warning sign and I didn't listen.

When the police pulled up, I was still performing CPR on Rich, but I knew that he was gone. I just didn't want to believe it. I wanted this to all be a dream.

"Hey, what's your name?"

"My name is Lillian."

"Could you step over this way with me, Lillian, and let the fellows do their job?"

I did as the officer said. He escorted me over to the patrol car where I had to sit in the back seat. I already knew he was taking me over to the patrol car to question me but I was not in the mood to answer any questions that he might have had. I was tired anyways, I needed to rest.

"Who did this, Lillian?" The officer got straight to the point.

"I don't know, I didn't get a look at the person that did it."

"Do you know if it was a man or woman?"

"No, I don't know."

"Well, how is this guy related to you?"

"We're not related at all; I was just in the area. I had just dropped my friend off to get her vehicle and then I was about to head home."

"So, you don't know this guy at all?"

"No, I don't know him," I replied, tears streaming down my face.

"You didn't see who murdered this guy?"

"No, I did not see anything." Even though the officer kept asking me the same questions just in different ways, my answers still remained the same and I still stayed solid.

"If we were to rewind the cameras back, we wouldn't see any foul play that you were involved in?"

"No, you wouldn't, officer, and if you would excuse me, I'm done answering questions. Any further questions you can take it up with my lawyer."

"Well, let me just tell you this, one of the officers pulled over a BMW and a girl by the name of TT was inside, and she told us *you* did it."

"She told you *what*? *I* did it? No way."

"Yes, she told it all and blamed *everything* on you. So do you mind if we test your hands for gunpowder residue?"

"No way, not without a warrant. I'm not doing any of that, there's no way anyone could tell you that I did this."

"How would I know her name then?"

"I don't know how you would know that, but I didn't do it."

My mind was going 100 mph. How did he know TT's name? Did she really tell the officer that I did it instead of taking responsibility for her own actions?

Here I was again going through the same thing I went through with Baby Girl. Instead, now, the shoe was on the other foot. I felt exactly how Baby Girl was feeling. All I could think about was that I couldn't go back. I couldn't go back to a jail cell and not have my freedom. I wasn't tripping about any surveillance cameras because I knew there weren't any, the only thing that puzzled me was how did the officer know that TT was in the area as well.

"Look, officer, like I said, I don't know anything and I'm about to leave, respectfully."

"All right, here's my card. I'll be in contact if I need anything else from you."

I nodded my head and walked away.

THIRTY
LILY

I sat in my car thinking; I couldn't believe this was happening to me again. *I didn't mean for any of this to happen. I didn't want it to go down like this*, was all I kept saying to myself. I lost my man because of my stupidity; all he wanted me to do was stay at home sometimes. Even though I wasn't out cheating on him with a nigga, I still cheated, and cheating was cheating. I sat in the parking lot crying my eyes out. I just couldn't move, I couldn't breathe. It was like my body was stuck in that seat. I was hoping the officer wouldn't come back over to my vehicle asking me any more questions before I got a chance to pull off but the way that I was feeling at that moment, he'd probably get cursed out.

A million ideas of how I could have done it differently went through my mind. After about an hour of sitting in the parking lot meditating, I decided to just leave and go home. Going home now wouldn't be the same because Rich wouldn't be there. A lot of crazy thoughts were traveling through my mind. I wanted to just go and put a bullet in TT's body or even my own body. My man's body had been riddled in bullets. She didn't have to shoot him that many times. Standing there seeing that happen all I could do was scream.

I called out for her to stop, but TT wouldn't listen as she kept spraying bullets. I loved Rich, with all my heart. There was no way that I was gonna leave him laid out there by himself. When I made it to my house, I walked inside, and it was pitch dark. I smelled a lot of weed smoke in the air, Rich must've been in here smoking a lot of blunts. I walked over to the chair where he always sat comfortably, seeing several bottles of liquor that were now empty.

My man was laying in here stressing over some shit that I was out doing, and he had no control of it, because I wanted to do what I wanted to do, and it only got me nowhere. I sat down in his favorite chair, laid my head back, and closed my eyes. He was just sitting in this exact spot getting fucked up. The more fucked up he had gotten, the more courage he had built up. He was so pissed off at me to the point where he had left the house to come looking for me.

I started feeling sick to my stomach. I ran to the bathroom and hovered over the toilet, but nothing seemed to come up. I was just gagging; it was just the thought of me just witnessing my man getting killed. There was no way that I was going to be able to stay in this house by myself at least for a few days. I went into the room and grabbed my bag, packed a few of my clothes, and got back in my car, driving to the nearest hotel.

When I arrived at the Marriott, the desk clerk already had an attitude due to the customer in front of me was giving her a hard time. I didn't want no smoke with her especially not after what I'd just been through. I was being very humble, but my mind was still not thinking too clearly, it had evil all over it. I just wanted to get my room and go lay down and thankfully, that was exactly what had happened. She still had a little attitude, but I was able to look over that because what she was going through wasn't my fault. But what I was going through I felt like *was* my fault and right now that's all that mattered to me.

THIRTY-ONE
LILY

I'd been back at the house for the past three days. It was weird with Rich not being there, but that was still my home. One day while I was in the living room watching TV someone knocked on my door. Looking in the peep hole I saw two detectives. One looked like Barney and the other one looked like Mr. Bean. At first, I wasn't going to open the door for these corny ass muthafuckas, but then I thought if I didn't open the door, that would make it seem like I had something to hide. Plus, I wanted to see what these clowns had to say now. I didn't want to speak with them before talking to TT because I still hadn't talked to her about the situation. She had been calling my phone every day since the incident but I wasn't in the mood to talk. I still wasn't sure if she really told those officers that I was the one that pulled the trigger. I was starting to think that she did because now they were knocking on my damn door. When I opened the door Barney walked in first.

"How may I help y'all?" I stood there nervously because I didn't know what to expect.

"Well, we are just following up on the murder that happened a few days ago that you were present at."

"Ok, what y'all want?" I asked nonchalantly.

"Well, what we want is an arrest."

"So y'all haven't found anyone yet?"

"No, and that is why we need you."

"Wait, y'all can't come in here like that, I'm not helping y'all get nobody. I told you I don't know who it was, I wasn't involved."

"It just seems a bit strange that you were just there. If I recall correctly, you said you were there taking your friend to get her car. Could you tell me your friend's name?"

"Look, I'm not about to give out no false information, I already told you I don't know nothing."

"Is her name Sky?"

Honestly, I didn't know what the bitch's name was, I just fucked her good pussy havin' ass and had a whole lot of fun teaming up with TT.

"I can't answer that."

"I'm asking because we have the cameras footage from that night and got her license plate number. We went over to Sky's house to have a conversation with her, and she told us that *you* committed the murder. Yeah, she told us *everything*; you thought she was gonna have your back, but she spilled the beans. So, if you don't want her to show up in court, testify against you, and help us get a conviction, we suggest you tell us your side of the story."

Oh, I know this piece of shit was lying because there weren't any cameras and I know damn well whatever the girl's name was did not tell him about no shit like that.

"I'm innocent. I didn't kill anyone."

"Forget having a pity party because we know everything.

Lillian, I pulled your records and I see that you were just in prison for robbery and murder, am I right?"

"Yeah, but so what? That's my past."

"I see that you are a lot humble now."

"I've always been humble until somebody fuck with me, but why we're bringing up my past? That has nothing to do with what happened a few days ago. I had absolutely nothing to do with that, I don't know who did it, so could you please leave out of my house."

Mr. Bean had nothing to say, fat boy did all the talking.

"If you would talk to us, we can help you."

"Help me for what? Why y'all trying to build a case on me? There's nothing you can stand here and tell me that's gonna make me admit that I was the one that murdered that man because I did not do it and I don't know who did it."

"But you just got out of jail for the same exact thing."

"No, it was not the same exact thing. Totally different situation happened in a different state, stop bringing up my past." I was getting mad now. Did they not understand that I'd just lost the move of my life? Here I was a grieving woman, and they were acting like *I* was the one who pulled the trigger.

"I'm going to ask you one more time, what was your involvement?"

"I'm telling you one more time, I had nothing to do with a murder."

"Alright then, pretty girl, you gonna look really good in orange again because you wanna play the tough role. I'm gonna leave my card here with you if you decide you wanna call me and save yourself from a whole lot of trouble," the officer spoke.

"When you decide you want to talk to me again, don't come by my house. You can take all the questions that you have to my lawyer."

"Enough said."

I immediately ran to my phone and called TT. I was ready to hear what she had to say. I knew those detectives didn't have anything on me because for once in my life, I was actually telling the truth. Except the part about me not knowing who Rich was, I just didn't want to get involved and get questioned further. Helping them further with their investigation was not an option for me, so I just stuck with the *not knowing him* lie.

When I called TT, she didn't answer, but not even three minutes later, my phone rang and it was her ass calling back.

"What's good? Why don't you answer my phone calls anymore?"

"You already know why; there's a lot been going on and I just had to get myself together mentally."

"But that shit didn't have nothing to do with you though."

"Well, let the investigators tell it, they said that you told them that I did it."

"They a fuckin' lie. Lily, please don't believe nothing that comes out of their mouths. Two officers pulled me over and asked me where I was coming from. I told them I was coming from the store getting gas. We didn't even have a conversation about you or the parking lot. Then they said they talked to the girl that was with us that night too."

"They are lying, don't believe them and don't talk to them again. You don't want to talk to them because you have nothing else to talk about. If they keep coming at you after you tell them that, you're going to lawyer up, that's harassment. So, keep it G and let's meet up soon… I miss you, I want to see you."

"Why do you feel like you can talk to me this way at a time like this?"

"We can be together now, babe," TT suggested. I could hear her smiling through the phone and I recoiled.

"Be together? I never wanted to be with you, TT… I told you that I wasn't going to leave my man. I may have dealt with you on the side, but I never was gonna leave my man for you, TT."

"Well shit, no strings attach, I still wanna see you."

"Just give me a few more days, let me get myself together and we can meet up."

"You want me to come by you?"

"No, you're not coming over here, it'll be the same routine, I will come see you."

"Okay babe, be like that then."

"Okay TT, bye. I'm just gonna hang up on you, TT."

This shit didn't faze TT at all, and I just couldn't have that type of person around me. I lost the love of my life and best friend because of this. Right now, I needed to stay on TT's good side because I needed to get close to Baby Girl again. Then, I would kill them both.

THIRTY-TWO
TT

Lily fucked my head up when she said she never planned to leave her boyfriend for me. All this time she was playing behind his back and lying to me. She was playing a dangerous game. That shit got her fucked over in the end, but had he not jumped out the car bussin', I would have never got spooked and started shooting back. I knew I could have just hit him in the leg or something small, but she gotta understand, I was scared for my life, so I went crazy. At the time I was shooting to kill, but I didn't know that was him rolling up on me like that.

Dude got out with some violent shit on his mind, he just should have been a lot smarter and thought that shit through. Never underestimate your opponent, you never know what they were capable of. I'd been studying Lily for a while now and she thought she was so smart but dumb as hell. I had a meet up with Jon Jon and Tiger before all of this went down, they told me about one of their opps who had just gotten out of prison and had moved to Atlanta.

As they kept talking, I found out the nigga they were talking about was Lily's boyfriend. When I told them I knew the chick that fuck with the nigga they were talking about, the niggas offered me $100,000 to give them the drop on the location. At first, I said *no* because I didn't want to do it. But then I thought about the money and agreed. I didn't even think about Lily's safety, but I was glad she was okay. Then when they got over there, the dude came out the house and did his thang, laying both of them down. I was tripping because they only paid me half and were supposed to give me the other half once the job was done. I was heated so I went by the warehouse and checked on my other half because it wasn't my fault that the niggas got laid down, I still wanted my shit.

When I stepped in there, I saw the same female that pulled up to my house for the pool party. Come to find out, her name was Baby Girl. I chopped it up with her and we became friends. From what she said about Lily, I could tell that it was a lot of animosity in the air. Some shit she tried to look over but wasn't healed yet, so I went with my move and got her on my team, filling her head up with all types of bullshit. I told her I was gonna look out for her because she used to fuck with that nigga Tiger, he was my lil' homie.

Baby Girl said she had my other half and that it wasn't right that they didn't give it to me all at one time. *That was her bad, being new to the streets, so I looked over that comment.* She told me to follow her to her crib. When we got there, she said, "Excuse the company; my stepmom lives with me, and my dad sometimes visits so he's probably in there too." So, I followed her inside and just as she said, they were both inside. Baby Girl introduced me to her mom first, and then her pops walked up and shook my hand.

Baby Girl immediately relayed to them that I knew Lily and

I'd been hanging around her lately, they were both in shock. Baby Girl informed me how it all started with Lily. I wasn't too shocked because I had already known the story; Lily had already laced me up on it awhile back. Her mom kept going on and on and on about how she wanted to kill Lily, so I already knew what time it was. They wanted me to get Lily in a bad spot so they could fuck over her.

Her pops were heated, and anger was built up inside of him too. Whatever happened between all of them in the past, I could tell the issue wasn't nearly over with. I followed Baby Girl upstairs, and she told me how she forgave her pops. Her pops had put her and her stepmother through so much, but they couldn't stop loving him as family. She said they were allowing him to come back and forth to visit and that she tried to forgive Lily. What Lily did to her was unforgettable. She told me some shit about how Lily was mad because her pops owed her some money and even years later, her pops went and met Lily to break even. And she promised not to stalk them again.

Baby Girl asked me had Lily ever said anything about her. I lied and told her *no* because I was fuckin' with Lily at the time, so I wasn't going to comment on what Lily had asked. So, I really just looked at Baby Girl as if she was speaking a language I didn't understand. She offered me another hundred bands to help them get Lily. Of course I complied. Baby Girl gave me her number and I wrote it down. I would hit her up, I wasn't sure if I wanted to do Lily wrong.

Now that I see that Lily wanna act brand new, the lil bitch wasn't as solid like how I thought she was, and she betrayed me. That nigga gone and she still don't wanna fuck with me now, so I was on some get back shit now. I was on some *fuck her* shit and was about to get this bag. I looked in my dresser drawer and got the white piece of paper where I wrote Baby

Girl's number on, sent her a text message from one of my burner phones, and she instantly replied.

Me: Wassup?

Baby Girl: Who dis?

Me: Dude from the other day, I told you I would hit you up.

Baby Girl: Oh yea.

Me: Unloyal ass hoe.

Baby Girl: I could have told you that.

Me: You did tell me that in so many words, all your people warned me. I just been so deep in with her for a while now and didn't want to believe it.

Baby Girl: So, what are we going to do about that? You know how I been feeling about the bitch.

Me: You should feel like that, you have every reason to.

Baby Girl: Yeah, that bitch tried to ruin my life, she really tried to end me.

Me: You didn't deserve any of that. What's the plan?

Baby Girl: You think you can get her in a spot by herself?

Me: That shouldn't be too hard, it may be a few days because she still in her feelings about some shit.

Baby Girl: Between me and you, I'm in my feelings too because I know all about what happened to Tiger and Jon Jon and I'm sure that bitch knows too. I believe she saw me from a distance, I gotta get her before she tries to get me.

Me: I would have known if she had plans to get at you, she doesn't know that I been talking to you. I lied, knowing damn well Lily wanted her top bad!

Baby Girl: Let's keep it that way then. I wanna beat that bitch's ass before I get rid of her.

Me: lol

Baby Girl: I think the warehouse would be a perfect spot to lay her down.

Me: That wouldn't work because I'm sure she has been out with Rich looking for Tiger and Jon Jon and they came across that spot.

Baby Girl: Yeah, you're right.

Me: Let's meet at my crib, it's quiet and out in the woods, nobody will hear us.

Baby Girl: Let her pick the day so she won't think nothing suspicious.

Me: Okay, I will drop my addy, when I text "pull up" that means everything is in place.

Baby Girl: I will see you soon.

I wasn't really tripping about texting Baby Girl because I was on a little burner phone. If shit went wrong, I could always deny that that shit wasn't mine. I just had to hit her up so we could get this shit in motion and put it on the floor. I really hated doing Lily like this, but at this point, she deserved it. She *asked* for it. I was unhappy about the way she'd been doing things. She was still living her best life, ignoring me and shit. Honestly, I wouldn't give a damn if Baby Girl killed Lily because she done already told me how the fuck she felt. She wasn't doing nothing differently and now it's like she done got worse since that nigga been gone.

Lily had gotten silent on me; I had been texting her first. When I asked her about coming over a few days ago she would have been excited to text me back. I knew it was over with, she stopped fuckin' with a nigga just like that. I wouldn't have any remorse for what she was about to receive. What Lily didn't realize was that she done hurt me so bad and she didn't know how I felt either when she left me almost every night to go home to that nigga.

You just didn't play with people's hearts like that because you never know what they were capable of doing. She done fucked with the wrong nigga's feelings this time though. I reached and got my other phone. Scrolling through the pictures and ran across a picture of me and Lily together. I couldn't believe I was this fucked up behind this bitch. I started thinking about all the evil things I could do to her; I could run her over, run her off the road, or even go burn the bitch's house down. I just wouldn't feel right taking her out like that though. The love of my life, my queen, that didn't care about me. I had to let her go.

THIRTY-THREE
LILY

TT had called me every day since the incident, she just wouldn't let me grieve in peace. My mind wasn't put back together for my good just yet, but I just had to get what I was feeling off my chest. So, when I called TT, she invited me over to her house, and this time, I didn't even put up a fight. She said it would just be only us two, and I was happy to hear that because honestly, I wasn't in the mood for any parties. I just wanted us to talk, get this shit off of our chests, and move on with our lives. I didn't know what I wanted to do with myself now that Rich was gone. Sad to say but when I was with Rich, he had it all figured out for our life.

We just had a few missions to complete before we could go back to being peaceful. I missed that man so much and I wished there was a way that I could call and tell him how sorry I was and apologize for everything that I put him through. All the bullshit I put that man through I made up my mind that I would just stay away from TT because when Rich was here, that's all he wanted was for me to stay home at night sometimes, with him. I owed it to him.

If TT tried to fuck me tonight, I was going to lie like my period was on. I just didn't want to have any dealings with her anymore. I knew everything that I had to tell her could be done over the phone, but she wanted to see me so bad, and this would be the perfect time to burst her bubble. I wasn't in the mood to snort any lines tonight, but I did take a few shots. After getting out of the shower I walked into my bedroom and glimpsed over at the dresser where Rich and I had our picture together sitting in a frame.

"Why did this have to happen?" I cried out. "I need you baby!" I grabbed my vibrator from out one of the dresser drawers and laid down on my back across the bed. Looking at my man's face, I began stroking my finger in and out of my wet pussy. I moved my body back and forth to the rhythm and took my finger out of my pussy and stuck it in my mouth to taste my own juices. I inserted my vibrator in and out and it felt so good against my pearl tongue.

The only person that was on my mind was Rich. He was the only one that could make me cum right now. I couldn't have him physically but mentally he was still all mine. I fucked the vibrator like it was my man's penis, even though my man's dick was way bigger than this shit. I called out Rich's name as if he was in the room. "Come for me, baby," he would tell me. I was in there playing both roles, in my mind, Rich was taking me on the ride of my life. If anyone was listening on the other side of my door, they would think I had lost my mind in here or probably would offer me an actress job because I played mine and Rich's roles really well.

As I began to cum, chills ran down my body, that shit was feeling so good to me. I knew I loved my man because he made me throw it back just by looking at his picture. I didn't want this episode to end, I was loving every moment. I was trying to hold my explosion as long as I could because I wasn't quite finished fantasizing about Rich. That imaginary 9-inch hard body was driving me crazy. I couldn't hold in any longer and exploded harder than ever! *Eww! I needed that,* I said to myself.

I got up from off the bed, the entire middle of my bed sheet was soaked and wet. I really wet my bed up that bad with a picture and a vibrator. I could barely walk to the bathroom but I was about to take another quick hot shower. I didn't care if I was late meeting TT. Fuck what she thought because it didn't fuckin' matter. I'd get there when I got there. Finished with my shower, I chose to wear a pair of skinny jeans, a T-shirt, and a pair of Jordans in case I had to stump a bitch tonight. I was hoping it didn't come down to that, I believed TT knew I was serious about cuttin' her off. If she tried to fuck me, I already had it on my mind to put her ass up.

TT didn't make me horny anymore and I wished I had realized that a long time ago instead of waiting too late. My man was gone now because I didn't realize what I had and appreciated what I had. It's okay though because I'm going to do the right thing now for my man. I grabbed my bag with my keys inside it along with my Glock and headed out the door.

Pulling up to TT's house, it was pitch dark, either she didn't pay her light bill or all the streetlights were out. I was getting a funny feeling about this and usually when I got a funny feeling, I would just leave; but it was something about *this* particular night that I couldn't leave or I just didn't want to. I called TT's phone before knocking on her door, but she didn't answer. I knew she was inside because her vehicle was parked. I opened my car door, turned on the light from my cell phone because it was too dark for me to even see to walk up the steps.

When I finally made it to the steps, I knocked on the door.

"Yo," I could hear TT say.

"It's me," I yelled back.

When she opened the door all I could see was a cloud of smoke, I knew she had been getting high.

"I called you, why you didn't answer?" I asked.

"I was in the kitchen, working us up a meal."

"Oh yeah, what you cook?"

"I cooked fried chicken, mac and cheese, Jiffy cornbread, and some Kool-Aid."

"Ok then, I'm ready to get my grub on."

I made it to the kitchen, sat down with TT, and she tried to offer me a line of coke. I declined it.

"Man, why you don't want no coke?" she asked, confusion all over her face.

"I'm good on that. I had a few shots already before I got here, I'm not trying to get too fucked up."

"A few shots? Shid, that never stopped you before; let me find out you are acting funny with me."

"What do you mean, let you find out, TT? I'm just over here to talk to you."

"Talk to me? I'm listening."

"Well, you know I've been going through a lot these past few days and it's a lot that I'm dealing with mentally. I lost my man and I understand that you don't care about that, TT, but you knew what my situation was when we got together. And I just want to make this thing right between us and not leave on bad terms."

"Naw, shid, we straight."

"No, we're not, TT, when you say stuff like that; that means you don't wanna hear anything I gotta say and you're gonna feel the way that you wanna feel. I'm over here trying to make this right with us."

"Can you just eat your food?"

"I can eat and talk to you at the same time."

"But that's not polite."

"You think everything is a joke, you're being sarcastic right now, stop doing that please. I want us to stop seeing each other as far as being sexual, not saying that I wanna end our friendship completely. I just wanna look at you as a friend and not a lover now."

"So why did you change your mind all of a sudden? Trying to make that nigga happy? He dead."

"You don't have to say it like that, I know he's dead; but I feel like I owe it to him, and I feel that he's still watching me."

"What, watching you? Come on, you can't be serious. You really think that nigga watching you?"

"Yes, he's in heaven."

"Man, Lily, when I met you, you were so gangsta, you had the style I looked for in all my women. I didn't know you had this type of soft shit in you tho, Lily. The Lily I know would have just eaten this shit up and moved on."

"That's the Lily that you used to know, but Rich did something to me; he brought out the best in me and he believed in me when nobody else did."

"So, you are saying I ain't believe in you, Lily?"

"Yes, you did but Rich and I had a different type of bond from what me and you had."

"Aight Lily, you wanna go… I'm going to let you go."

"But I still wanna be friends."

"Nah, I can't be friends with somebody that I once fucked on and had feelings for, where they do that at? You do not see my point of view either. You mislead me to think you fucked with me the long way."

"Okay, you're so hard to talk to and get you to understand where I'm coming from."

"Yeah whatever, I don't care to know where you're coming from."

"Alright, enough said. Um… I need to use the bathroom."

"Go to the one upstairs."

I went upstairs to the bathroom because I needed to get away from TT for a second. Going into the bathroom I stood and looked into the mirror and just threw water on my face. I was relieved that part of telling her how I felt was over with. Walking out of the bathroom, I could hear TT downstairs on the phone telling somebody that she was on the way to the door now.

She had told me that there was nobody else joining us, that it would just be us two. So, I waited before walking down the steps to see who was joining us. I became nervous when I peeped around the corner and saw Baby Girl, Alice, and Jonathan standing there in the living room.

"What the fuck is going on?" I yelled, looking over at TT. "What the fuck are you doing?" I continued.

All I could think about was the fact that TT had set me up. They were all here together. There's no way they were here to be friendly. I was trying to find a way out but there was no way out. Going back up the stairs, I tried the window, but it was too high for me to jump. I had left my purse downstairs with my Glock in it, so I was in a fucked-up situation. I had to think fast. Should I just go down there and act like I didn't know anyone was in the house or should I just toughen up and remind myself of all the fucked-up things I'd done in my life? I didn't have to pee at first but now I had to, so I rushed back to the bathroom, sat on the commode until finally I let out a drizzle, flushed, and washed my hands.

I ran back out, still pacing the floor until I heard someone shout, "Lily, you might as well stop running and face your fate. I told you Karma was a bitch."

"Really, TT?" I yelled out in anger while deciding to take my chance, retracing my steps back down the stairs, and entering the living room – or should I say firing squad? I didn't understand how she could do something like this to me. Even more importantly, how had I not noticed that she was playing me? I was angry with both her and myself.

"Man, I don't wanna hear nothing you gotta say, you fucked me over. I just had to get my lick back."

"You really set me up with these clowns?"

"This is a setup for revenge, baby."

"Hold your horses, Lil' Mama, I'm not the same Baby Girl that you knew years ago… the Baby Girl from years ago would just sit on her hands and let you lead the way. The Baby Girl that I am today will put bullet holes in you right now. I learned a thing or two from dealing with some street niggas."

I eased over to the love seat where my Glock was in my bag. As soon as I got the chance, I would reach for it. "Oh yeah, so what y'all want with me?" I asked, backing up closer to my purse.

"It's been a long-time coming, Lily, you set out revenge on my Baby Girl here. You almost sent her away for a very long time," Jonathan threw out there, reminding me of my past transgression.

"But didn't we just have a conversation about leaving your *family* alone?"

"Yeah, but it was too easy when this opportunity presented itself. I *had* to renege on our agreement."

"I wasn't fuckin' with y'all, so you come fuckin' with me?"

"We didn't mean for it to happen like this, the opportunity just fell into our laps."

"Yeah Lily, what you gotta say now?" Alice yelled.

I hurried and grabbed my Glock from my bag and shot TT in her stomach. Then I felt a bullet hitting me in my leg.

"What the fuck?! You shot me bitch!" TT yelled.

I was on the floor holding my leg as TT called me every name in the book. I could hear her trying to catch her breath in between curse words. "That's for Rich!" I screamed. "That's for betraying me." I yelled again.

"It seems like déjà vu, huh, Lily? I remember I was in this *exact* situation a few years ago. Helpless, I didn't know what would happen next. What you put me through had me scared for a very long time. I didn't have friends for a very long time. I couldn't trust anyone."

"Bitch, you played me, you took me for granted. I was innocent, you tried to make me look like the bad guy, you didn't take full responsibility for your own actions, instead you left me there to take all the charges. You knew I was trying to get my life together, all I wanted to do was put my past behind me, finish school, and make it out the trenches. I depended on you, we did *everything* together, and the whole time you were *a snake*. You tried to corrupt my image and make me look like something that I wasn't. You tried to take my freedom from me, and you sat back and laughed like the shit was funny. But what you did, didn't stop me. You didn't stop the woman that I am today. You didn't stop my coins. You didn't stop my life. And I forgive you. I'm sad to say this, Lily, but you *will* die here today. I was dead inside for years."

"I don't give a damn about that, I lost *the best thing* that ever happened to me, so I guess I'll just be joining him."

"*You* put *our sweet Baby Girl* in a situation, knowing she was already going through something," Alice told me.

"When I met her, *you two* made sure that she was already scarred. I didn't do any more damage to her than what she was already feeling inside," I declared, looking at Alice and Jonathan.

"That's my family, Lily, I forgave them; they didn't come close to doing what you did to me, you were trying to send me away to jail for life. This should teach you a lesson about fuckin' over someone so close to you and that has *never* did you any harm. I had your back, I gave you a place to sleep, and I gave you food to eat. I should have killed you the first day I saw you."

Click. Click. Click. "Fuck… my gun is jammed!" Baby Girl yelled.

I struggled while trying to get up and reach for my gun that slid up under the love seat. Baby Girl grabbed my feet. I fought her back, but I wasn't strong enough. When I finally got a good grip on her, I felt a bullet hit me right between the eyes. TT had shot me.

As I crossed over to the other side, Rich welcomed me into his arms. *"My Lily, you have come to be with me, you couldn't battle those storms. Don't worry, you are in good hands now and forever. Everything has worked itself out for the better. I looked down upon you and saw that you were as loyal as ever. I was smiling ear to ear; you had gotten as soft as a feather, I knew that you couldn't stay away, my dear. You were betrayed by someone you thought had your back, but the whole time, she was out seeking revenge."*

THE END!

REVIEWS

Did you enjoy the read?
Let us know how much by leaving us a review on Amazon and
Goodreads.

OTHER BOOKS BY
URBAN AINT DEAD

Tales 4rm Da Dale

The Hottest Summer Ever

Hittin' Licks For The Holidays: Atlanta

Wet Dreams On Lockdown: The Nurse

How To Publish A Book From Prison

By **Elijah R. Freeman**

Despite The Odds

By **Juhnell Morgan**

Good Girls Gone Rogue 1 & 2

By **Manny Black**

Hittaz 1, 2, 3, & 4

Coldhearted 1 & 2

By **Lou Garden Price, Sr.**

Charge It To The Game 1 & 2

A Summer To Remember With My Hitta

Snatched Up By A Hitta

Santa Sent Me A Real One For Christmas

Wet Dreams On Lockdown: The Unit Manager

Thug Me The Right Way 2 & 3

Seizing A Gangsta's Heart For The Summer

By **Nai**

A Setup For Revenge

Wet Dreams On Lockdown: The Librarian

By **Ashley Williams**

Ridin' For You

Ridin' For You, Too

Trickin' On A Heaux For Christmas

Homie Hoppin' For The Holidays

Wet Dreams On Lockdown: The Female C.O

Letters Of His Love

By **Telia Teanna**

The State's Witness 1, 2 & 3

This Time Won't You Save Me 1 & 2

His Summer Side Piece

By **Kyiris Ashley**

Stuck In The Trenches 1 & 2

By **Huff Tha Great**

The Swipe

By **Toōla**

Melted The Heart Of A Menace

Wet Dreams On Lockdown: Lieutenant Grace

By **P. Wise**

Merry Trapmas

By **Mia Sky**

Thug Me The Right Way

By **DiamondATL & Nai**

Wet Dreams On Lockdown: The Counselor

By **Paris Iman**

Wet Dreams On Lockdown: The Male C.O

By **Tamyra Griffin**

Wet Dreams On Lockdown: The Captain

By **TN Jones**

Wet Dreams On Lockdown: The Warden

By **Shawnice**

Atlantastan 1 & 2

By **Chris Green**

IN The Streetz

By **Tron Hill**

BOOKS BY
URBAN AINT DEAD'S C.E.O

<u>Elijah R. Freeman</u>

Triggadale 1, 2 & 3

Tales 4rm Da Dale

The Hottest Summer Ever

Murda Was The Case 1, 2 & 3

Hittin' Licks For The Holidays: Atlanta

Wet Dreams On Lockdown: The Nurse

How To Publish A Book From Prison

STAY CONNECTED

Follow Elijah R. Freeman
On Social Media
FB: Elijah R. Freeman
IG: @the_future_of_urban_fiction